TRIUMPHS

&

TRAGEDIES

By Tashema Chanel

Printed in the United States of America. First printing, 2019, Lulu.com.

ISBN: 978-0-578-21750-5

Book cover designed by Savant MEDIA Group, LLC, a digital media company.

Love exists when you are ready to receive it.
In the meantime, don't be deceived.

"When someone shows you who they are, believe them - the first time."
-- Maya Angelou

Ashley
Because of You
"I'm kind of stuck between my fantasy and what is real" - NeYo

Taylor's number popped up on my screen again. I ignored it as I ran to baggage claim. I spotted my luggage and reached for the handle. I struggled to pull it off the conveyor belt but eventually managed to grab my suitcase-on-wheels off the belt before it looped around again. Ray, who stood up against a pillar as he charged his cell phone, chuckled.

"What's so funny? I could've used your help," I said as I walked up to him. Ray rested his arm on my shoulder as we walked through the automatic doors to the sidewalk. Taylor called again. I answered the call as I caught sight of her Audi truck in the distance. As we walked toward Taylor's car, Manny Money and two older white men, dressed in gray, pinstripe business suits with their briefcases in hand, cornered Ray.

"How was Vegas?" Manny asked Ray.

"How are you guys doing today?" Ray asked. He held his hand out for a handshake that no one accepted.

"How was Vegas?" Manny repeated sternly. Ray did not respond. Each of the three men stood idle, glaring at Ray, whilst glancing at each other. They all remain`1ed in silence. I watched the tense exchange as I put my bags in the trunk. Ray frowned as he attempted to think of a valid excuse to give his bosses as to why he was in Vegas, knowing he wasn't allowed to go. Ray opened his mouth to answer when Manny put his hand up in the air.

"Save it for the ride," Manny said as he walked toward a black Scion truck with Manny's promotional photo for Blaze 101.1 FM plastered along the side of it. "You can tell me all about how Vegas was on the way to the station. We're headed to the station now, Ray. Hop in," Manny said, holding the back door open for Ray.

"I'll see you at the house later," Ray said to me. He hesitated to give me a kiss in front of his bosses, so I simply nodded and waved goodbye as I hopped in the front seat of Taylor's SUV and greeted my best friend with a hug.

"How was Vegas?" Taylor asked as she pulled off. I fastened my seatbelt. "You guys didn't get married - did you?" Taylor looked at me from the corner of her eye as she eased into bumper-to-bumper traffic. I smirked and temporarily ignored the question. I glanced in the back seat for a peek at Isaiah, who was asleep. His head rested on the side of his booster seat and drool dripped from the side of his mouth.

"I'm still high from that west coast air. How was Izzy his first full week away from his mom," I asked.

"Girl, you were the last person on Isaiah's mind. He had a blast. You know Poppa Jax and G-ma Amy are with him; their first grandchild. Isaiah was spoiled rotten from the moment he hit the door," Taylor responded. "Isaiah ate chocolate chip cookies for breakfast, birthday cake ice cream for lunch and candy for dinner."

"They always show him a good time. Don't forget to tell them I said thank you."

"I won't...you already know how my parents are. But don't change the subject. I want the juice about Vegas." I laughed.

"Vegas was fun. We really enjoyed ourselves," I said. I smiled then realized Kaila, Taylor's four-year-old daughter, was wide awake. I giggled at my smiling goddaughter and handed her a pink flamingo Beanie baby. "And no, I didn't get married. Yet."

"Hallelujah!" Taylor raised her hands in the air. "Thank God!"

"Really? Why are you so excited that your best friend *didn't* get married?"

7

"I'm happy you didn't *rush* into marriage with someone you barely know. Trust me, marriage is not for the faint."

"I'm not even sure how to take that..." I replied in disbelief. "But I did enjoy Vegas. It was lit. And I won some money."

"Yes! Get that money, honey," Taylor said. "I can't believe it. I knew you would, you lucky bitch. I've been hating since the day you *won* those tickets," Taylor said with a smirk. Taylor's insinuation was that I didn't actually win the tickets at all, but rather, Ray, who was in charge of calling out the winning raffle ticket called my ticket number because his intentions were always to win me over. Taylor, like everyone else at Blaze's annual Labor Day cookout, thought Ray tampered with the results of the raffle - and said so every chance she has gotten since I won.

"Who wouldn't enjoy an all expense paid trip to gamble for free," Taylor said. "I haven't been on vacation since...my honeymoon," Taylor said with a hint of nostalgia in her voice.

"I won $1,000 off of putting $20 in slots!" I added. "Technically, I didn't lose any money. I gambled my winnings so I really just broke even. I don't need to waste any more money with this wedding coming up." Taylor didn't respond to the wedding planning chatter. "And I'm sure Chris has something nice in store for you for Valentine's Day. That's right around the corner."

"We shall see," Taylor said with low-key sorrow.

"Where is Chris at now," I asked.

"Working," Taylor said. "Per usual," she added. "You know he's been working double shifts every day this month? Every freaking day. He usually works four days on with three days off. On his days off from the fire department, Chris works at the hospital as a first-responder from Sunday to Tuesday. And to make matters worse, he's been doing per diem shifts at the department so, I never see him. I wake up super early or wait up late for him just to get see his face. On his days off he's too tired to do anything besides play with Kaila or hang out at his momma house." Taylor quickly became tight-lipped and gazed out the window, depressing herself even more with overthinking.

"We set a date!" I blurted out. The random exclamation was a way to change the subject. "I'm so excited to jumpstart our wedding plans," I enthused. "Because in six months, I'll be Mrs. King." I beamed with glee as I stared down at my engagement ring. Taylor sighed but remained quiet. She failed to offer a congratulations or ask for details. "We're getting married in December!"

"Good for you," Taylor whispered eventually. She followed her bland congratulations up with her unsolicited advice. "You shouldn't rush to plan a wedding if he can't trust you." I rolled my eyes and sighed heavily. Taylor brought me down from cloud nine - as only she could.

"What are you talking about now?" I asked a snarky Taylor. "Why am I untrustworthy?"

"You know you're my girl so I'm always going to keep it real with you," Taylor explained. "I don't think it's fair that you are keeping secrets from your fiancé. I know you didn't tell him yet."

"Of course I didn't," I said hastily. "Um, the subject really didn't come up," I said.

"You are the one who can bring it up," Taylor said. "I'm sure Ray wondered why he didn't get to hit those skins while you were in Vegas."

"I got this under control. I'm celibate - that's why," I said. I'm still trying to convince myself that was the actual reason. "Don't even go there Taylor, please. You know I'm not even really trying to get caught up with Ray."

"You guys are planning a wedding, setting dates and what not. It sounds like he already caught you."

"Ray is a player, has always been one...may always be one. I'm merely waiting for the right moment to tell him. And I will. Until I feel like he's not playing me - then I will tell him."

"It's not right Ashley," Taylor said. "That's all I'm saying. You're being just as deceitful as..."

"Don't even go there," I said, cutting her off mid-sentence. I looked directly in her face - daring Taylor to utter his name. "Don't do it, Taylor."

"Jay-J," she blurted. I rolled my eyes like the girl's head turned in the Exorcist and crossed my arms like an upset toddler. *The bitch went there. Typical Taylor.*

"I'm nothing like Jay-J," I said. "And, I'm actually insulted at the comparison. There are many reasons why I'm not like Jay-J. But I'd think the biggest difference is that I'm not having sex with Ray, pretending to be single, while planning a wedding with someone else for starters."

"But you are planning a wedding and you aren't being honest. It sounds too similar to what Jay-J did to you," Taylor said. "You aren't really going to go through with this whole wedding planning process just for the wedding to not happen because of a secret, will you? What if you end up lying to the man who really loves you?"

"Since when did you become Ray's cheerleader all of a sudden?" I quipped. "It's a swift change from your normal spew of hate you have for him." Taylor pulled into the driveway of my Briarwood townhome. Before the car was fully stopped, I jumped out the front seat and unloaded my belongings from the trunk. I left the bags at the door as I loaded my most precious cargo into the house. I returned to the front door to thank Taylor for the ride home and her babysitting duties.

"I just want you to be happy, Ashley Jay," Taylor said. "You can't have happiness harboring secrets that can destroy it."

"Happiness is all relative, Taylor. Not everyone can talk like best friends and be freaks with each other like you and Chris," I said as I wheeled my luggage into the house. "Those are real relationship goals."

"Yeah, whenever he's not working," Taylor replied. "It's great. We're great."

"Thanks again for everything, even your concern," I said. "No matter how unnecessary."

"No problem," Taylor said as she backed out of the driveway. She honked her horn and waved before she pulled off down the street.

Back inside, I undressed Isaiah and put his pajamas on. As I tucked him into his bed my phone rang. I checked the caller ID and Chris's number showed up.

"What's up Chris?" I answered.

"Did Taylor pick you up yet? I just called her but she didn't answer," Chris said.

"She sure did. She just left my house," I said. "You're still at work?"

"No, I got off early. I wanted to surprise my lady with a date." Chris always had a romantic streak. Taylor didn't realize how lucky she was.

"She literally just left. She didn't mention she was going anywhere so she should be home soon." Although, Taylor didn't mention going straight home either.

"Oh, how was Vegas?" Chris asked.

"It was awesome. I'd pay to go next time," I said. We both laughed.

"You may not have to. I'm planning something special for me and Taylor's anniversary that might involve a trip. I'll keep you posted."

"Oh, sounds intriguing," I said. My other line rang as we chatted. I checked the caller ID. It was Morgan.

11

"I gotta go Chris. My best friend is calling. I'll text Taylor. But I'd give her fifteen minutes. She should be by then."

"Ok. Thanks, Ashley," Chris said. "Bye."

"Later dude," I said before switching lines.

"What's up boo?" I asked my friend since college.

"How was Vegas? You're not married are you?" Morgan asked.

"Funny," I said with a chuckle. "No. I'm not married. Vegas was great, actually. Extremely relaxing."

"That is not enough information. You know I want details," Morgan said. "I need them! How was the weather? Did you sightsee? Did you get drunk? Did y'all do it?"

"The journalist in you comes out," I said. "All these damn questions. Let me get a glass of wine." I filled my flute glass to the brim and sat back on the couch and divulged about my week in Vegas with Ray.

"You would never guess who I ran into at Toca on Friday," Morgan said.

"Who?"

"Travis," Morgan said giddily. I rolled my eyes.

"What was he talking about?" I asked.

"You," she said. I couldn't help but blush. Just the mention of his name could always bring me back. Travis always had that effect on me.

"What about?" I asked. "I can't see what could have been said. Travis and I haven't spoken since he told me he had a baby with Corrine."

"Well, you know he heard about your engagement." The grand spectacle Ray caused when he proposed earlier this year had everyone talking. It was in the paper, on the radio and of course posted to onblast.com.

"And I bet he was full of heartbreak," I said sarcastically.

"He wasn't happy about it," Morgan said. "He was so concerned with your reasoning for choosing Ray."

"Travis could feel whatever way about whomever. He chose Corrine. Remember? Did you remind him of that?" I said peeved.

"I did. All Travis maintained about Corrine was that she's a good mom. He was more interested in talking about you, Ray and you're wedding. Travis spoke more of Ray and his reputation than anything else.

"Travis is baffled that you would deal with Ray when he's a known cheater. You already know Ray does have a little name for himself around Providence."

"Well, luckily for Travis, there's no nice way to say, 'mind your business,' you know?" I said. "And besides that, who Ray has sex with is none of my business."

"Bih!" Morgan exclaimed. "What do you mean? That's your fiancé," Morgan reminded me.

"But I'm not his wife, so it's none of my business until it is."

"That's the stupidest thing I've ever heard you say, "Morgan said. "And yet, I get it."

"That's why you're my best friend. So when are we linking up?"

"Ladies Night is at my house this time. I'm on assignment this week and next week. My mom wants to go to Mohegan the following weekend so I'm not free until...How about the weekend of March 19th? That's a Saturday. Are you working?"

"That's in about a month," I said as I checked my calendar. "I'm scheduled for a 12-hour shift but I get off at seven in the evening so that works."

13

"Don't forget to tell Taylor. You know how she acted the last time it was at my place. And my friendliness can only take so much," Morgan said. "She can keep that Riverside attitude over there in Riverside."

"I will prepare Taylor. She'll be fine," I reassured my friend. "You guys are wearing out my peacemaking skills."

"It's not her I'm worried about. I don't need anymore jail time," Morgan said with a laugh.

"You've never been to jail," I said, shaking my head.

"And I'm not trying to go. Not on account of Miss Prissy," Morgan said. "You better talk to your girl."

"Relax, Morgan. Count to ten or something," I said. "We are *all* friends. But I will talk to Taylor about her hassadiddy and sarcastic comments. But in the meantime, I'm going to jump in the shower and get this travel funk off me."

"Ok. I'll give you a call in the middle of the week to confirm. Don't book any overtime - you know - if you can help it."

"You know how the emergency room is - unpredictable. Let's talk Wednesday to see what are schedules are looking like."

"Cool. I'll talk to you soon, boo," Morgan said.

"Bye," I said. I walked into the bathroom and let the water run. The bathtub filled as I undressed. I received a message from Ray. "On my way," it said. I went to text him back to ask him to bring me some Chinese when another message came through. "With your favorite takeout."

"Can't wait," was my reply. Twenty minutes later Ray walked through the door with a chicken lo mein dinner in his hand. While not my first choice, it was a good choice. Ray greeted me with a kiss.

"We need to talk," Ray said sternly. He left the food in the plastic bag. He dropped the bag on the table and began to pace through the living room. "Manny wasn't too happy to see me at the airport."

"What happened? What did he say? You didn't get fired did you?" I asked knowing Ray was used to getting away with a lot because of how close Manny had been to Ray's father. When Ray's father died, Manny promised to look out for Ray, Rochelle and Richie. Ray should have known his job would be in jeopardy when he had Mikey overlook Ray's name on the flight and hotel reservations.

"No, Manny didn't do much of the talking. He introduced me to one of the corporate accountants of the firm. That's how he found out I was on the flight reservation and at the hotel. The accountant ran my name against payroll. They said it was a standard process." Ray continued as I made his dinner plate. "You already know I had a story for him, but Manny told me to save it. The other dude was Manny's boss, the director of promotional events. He said I had better shape up or I could be fired. So I'm safe for now."

"Oh my goodness. That's crazy. I can decide who I want to take with me. They didn't have a stipulation for me."

"That's why you're not the one getting punished," Ray quipped. "According to Manny, I knew the rules and tried anyway."

"I'm sorry Ray," I said. I rubbed his shoulder and kissed him on the cheek. "Let's eat and I'll try to make you relax." I kissed his neck. Ray leaned his head back and closed his eyes. He let out a small moan.

"It took all this for me to get some? I should get in trouble more often," he said with a devilish grin.

"Who said anything about you getting some? You're not tasting this cookie until I'm the only one left in the jar. I said I'd make you relax."

"Sex would make me relax," Ray huffed as he folded his arms like an upset six-year-old.

15

"Try again Raymond," I said. I managed a smile so I wouldn't damper his mood too much more. "You know my rule Ray. It's the only one I got."

"I know," Ray said sullenly. "No sex until the wedding. It's fine," he moped. Ray's mood seem to illuminate. "It better be one hell of a wedding night," he added. Ray slapped my butt and smiled his dimpled smile. He was so gorgeous. Nearly irresistible. I bit my bottom lip. "Don't do that," he said with a laugh, grabbing my waist. "You little tease," he said as he pulled me closer into his body.

"Stop it," I said. "I told you it was going to be tough. You'll make it through. I have faith in you." We laughed and finished dinner with talks of wedding details. Ray washed the dishes and I dried them. I put them in the mahogany cabinets above the sink.

As we watched reruns of *Martin* on the sofa, I snuggled close to Ray. He wrapped his muscular arms around me. We lay twisted together like a pretzel. I laid my head on his chest as he breathed in the scent of my hair.

"Coconuts?" he asked. He ran his fingers through strands of my hair slowly. "It's gotta be coconuts."

"You're right," I said. *Attentive.* I smiled as he kissed my forehead. I looked up. We faced each other now. I poked out my lips, puckering for a kiss. He leaned forward, obliging. I pushed my left hand out and gazed at my ring. I smiled and tucked my hand back under his body. As he breathed my body moved in sync with his motions.

I hesitated to bask in my newfound happiness. I couldn't help but wonder if this time was real. I had this seeping feeling that inevitability was on its way into this relationship. I just didn't know when the other shoe would drop. But I was expecting it. "You know...I'm not too big on trust," I explained to Ray. "Especially men. I've learned too much about how they operate. In order for this to work, like really work out, I need this to be real. I need you to be real."

"Of course this is real," Ray said as he hugged me tighter. "Come on. I'm King Ray. I don't know how to be anything else. You should know by now that I love you, Ashley."

"Love is not something you just say - you have to show it," I said. "A lot of girls would be mad if this wasn't real. So if it's not -"

"It's real," Ray said. "And I'm ready." I kissed him back to offer my regression. I know Ray. And Ray isn't the faithful type. He may love me but is how he feels *now* enough? Enough to handle the truth? Enough to be faithful? I'm not sure if he's ready for a real relationship -- let alone marriage. And who am I to stop him from cheating?

Some guys are faithful but most guys are not. At least not the ones I've met. Yet Ray wants me to believe that he is faithful - or that he is willing to be for me. I feel like Ray is trying to convince me that he's actually done a complete 180 instead of actually doing one.

Unfortunately for Mister Raymond King, Miss Ashley is not convinced. You know what they say, once a cheater, always a cheater. So this is all a test.

Let Ray tell it...everything is perfect. Despite what Ray shares with others to boost his ego or keep up his playboy image, Ray hasn't tasted my sweetness just yet. And only if he passes this test will he get to. When I know this relationship with Ray is real is when I will let him completely in. But until then, my secret will stay my little secret.

Ray
Un-thinkable

"This is exactly how it should feel when it's meant to be. And I deserve it." - Alicia Keys

The heavy glass, wooden-framed door took more force to open it than I expected. The hostess directed me to the bar counter to pick up my takeout order. To the left, Alana came through the revolving kitchen door to the dining area with a tray of drinks in her hand. Alana served the table of three young girls, who looked like they were skipping school. She glanced at the wall mirror and fixed her fly-away hairs before Alana made her way to the bar area.

"Alana, boo. How have you been?" I asked. Alana smiled her usual buck-toothed grin. "Somebody's been eating well." I grabbed an inch of Alana's love handles and jiggled it.

"Yeah, when you work for Harry's Bar & Burgers, it's easy to put on a couple of pounds, especially eating chocolate crack everyday," Alana confessed as she pulled away from me.

"Who would've thought that the unthinkable would have happened," a familiar voice bellowed out from behind me. "My boy Ray done popped the question," Mikey said with a handshake-turned-hug.

"And somebody besides the infamous crazy Stacy said yes," Alana responded to Mikey. "Congratulations," she said to me with her arms extended for a hug. "It's very hard to believe that just six months ago we were sexing on a daily basis."

"The King is retiring his player card," Mikey added. "I still can't believe it, man. You out of all people. Who knew I would live to see the day," he said with a smile.

"The day will come soon enough. She's the one, and when you know...you know," I replied. "She makes me happy - I just want to do the same for her."

"I hope she knows how lucky she is to have you Ray," Alana complemented sarcastically as she checked on my takeout order at the small window between the kitchen and its serving area.

"I'm the lucky one, La," I replied. "The last six months have been life changing."

"Yeah, for everybody," Alana said.

"Ashley is really an amazing person," I gushed.

"Good. I'm glad someone was able to tame your wild ass. I can't believe you're really off the market. I hope you do Ashley better than you did Stacy - or me for that matter." Alana tried to play busy by folding napkins.

"What are you talking about, 'La? You know you and I had an understanding."

"What was that understanding?" Alana asked with her hand on her hip.

"You understood that Stacy was my girlfriend at the time and I understood that you didn't care that Stacy was my girl." Alana shook her head no. She gathered the folded napkins and placed them on her tray in between two clean glasses and a set of silverware.

"The only thing I understood was even though Stacy was your girl, she couldn't keep you satisfied. And that's why you were always trying to fuck me. I can't understand why Stacy was your girl in the first place," Alana said as she wiped down the small dining table. She placed the folded napkins, glasses and silver onto the tabletop. The service bell rang and the chef yelled, 'Order up.' Alana walked behind the bar and the bag of takeout and handed it to me.

19

"And I can't for the life of me understand why you always bring up Stacy. My relationship with her had nothing to do with my friendship with you - but that's an unthinkable concept you have yet to comprehend. Can you hand me some wet wipes?"

"I can't understand why you would lie about having a girlfriend," Alana said as she rolled her eyes. She grabbed and handful and tossed them to me.

"I can't understand why you would believe otherwise," I countered. "Look at me, 'La. Why wouldn't I have a girl?" I said as I walked toward the exit.

"I believed you because I wanted to. I wanted you." Alana paused then shook her head. "It doesn't matter. We'll be forever connected."

"Your crazy is showing, 'La," I said with a chuckle. "Walk me to the car," I said to Mikey. "Have a good day, Alana." I grabbed my to-go bag, waved and walked away. Outside, Mikey and I stopped at Ashley's four-door black Acura.

"Boy, that girl is still stuck!" I said to Mikey as I unlocked the doors, remotely. "I really wish Alana would find a hobby or something; workout a little bit more and try to focus on something other than my life."

"That's your fault, bro," Mikey said. "You strung her along for years. I'm surprised Alana is taking this so well."

"This?" I questioned. "Should I get your soapbox out? I hear a lecture coming on."

"You're really going to go through with this?" Mikey asked when he sat in the passenger's seat.

"There's that *this* again. What are you referring to? Me finally taking your advice by maturing and getting serious about one woman? I told you when I saw her that she was the one," I proclaimed.

"Lucky for you, I haven't had any lady juices in that bed for a while now. You're safe," I joked. It was nice to have this version of Shirley back.

"Well, that Ashley girl has had a positive effect on you," Shirley noted with a smile. Shirley disappeared in my room as I kicked back and watched tv. Two movies later, I got the call from Ashley to come through.

"I'm headed to Ashley's," I yelled out to the family as I left the house. "Don't wait up."

I pulled into Ashley's garage and entered her house. I put the keys on the end table outside of the hall door and strolled through the quiet townhouse. I called out to my future wife.

"Bae," I shouted out. "Where are you?"

"In the kitchen" she replied. I walked through the swinging door between the dining room and kitchen. Ashley stood in front of the stove stirring a red pot. Her hips swayed with her circular motion. She turned her head towards me. All I saw was those big hazel eyes of hers. I smiled. She smiled back.

"So what do you think about red roses? Red as an accent color?" She asked. Bridal magazine spreads were scattered over the small dinette table in the corner. "I've been looking for a basic color that all of my bridesmaids will look good in."

"It's whatever you want," I said and kissed her cheek. I sat down on the stool at the dinette table.

"You always say that," she said, bringing me a spoonful to taste.

"That's always going to be my answer so you should start believing it," I said as I threw a thumbs up to the chef.

"I'm starting to believe it," she said with a smile. She stared at me but looked as though her thoughts were miles away. "I love you Ray," she said sweetly.

23

"I love you too," I replied. "Where's Isaiah?"

"He's with my mom and Harold," Ashley answered as she set the dining room table. "Tomorrow I'm going into work at 7. I'm working a 12-hour shift then going to Morgan's for ladies night."

"Ladies Night, huh?" I asked, interested in what really happens when women get together in groups. "What are you going to do?"

"It's at Morgan's house on Broadway, downtown Providence. We'll be lucky to make it into her apartment without a proposition."

"Sounds like my kind of night," I said as I finished up the remaining scraps of food on my plate. Ashley went into the bathroom for a quick shower.

"You would hate our ladies night - besides the food, it's just me and my girls gossiping about our lives, trying to figure out our next power move. We talk money goals and irritating work situations," Ashley said as she dried her damp body with an oversized gray towel. She lotioned her legs, bent over with the towel wrapped around her waist. I walked up behind her to assist.

"Let me get that spot you missed," I said as I lathered a handful of lotion onto her bare back. "You can't tease me like this." I rubbed her back, caressed her arms and kissed her shoulder as she fastened her black lace bra.

"You're making this harder on yourself," Ashley said as she inched away to clothe the rest of her body. She slipped her panties on underneath her bath towel. The towel fell to the floor revealing Ashley's voluptuous shape. I thrust my pelvis into her backside. Ashley looked back at me and frowned. "Ugh," she sighed. "Do you mind giving me a little space?" Ashley bumped me with her butt, pushing me back onto the bed.

"I liked that," I revealed. I rubbed Prince until he was hard. "You think you could hook a brother up?" I glanced at Ashley, down at Prince then back up at Ashley. She shook her head from side to side.

24

'No," she whispered. "I had a long day." Ashley put on knee-length, polka-dot socks, a pair of NOIR capri sweats and white NOIR tank top. She propped two pillows up behind her and leaned back against the headboard.

"Let me hook you up then," I said as leaned in to kiss Ashley. She kissed back, passionately. I kissed her neck. I kissed the part of her breasts that were exposed. Ashley moaned a pleasure whisper. I kissed Ashley again and moved my way downtown. Ashley grabbed my face into both of her hands.

"No," she said sternly. "No sex until we're married." I rolled over, rolled my eyes and repeated, 'really' almost inaudibly. I sighed heavily.

"It's a proven fact that sex declines after marriage. Let's not become a statistic," I said. I added a smile, knowing my dimple will have its usual effect. Ashley rolled her eyes.

"Why do we have to keep talking about something we already agreed to? It's frustrating and annoying."

"So is blue balls," I countered.

"Well that's your problem for rubbing on me as soon as I got out of the shower." I poked Ashley with the pitched tent under my gray boxer briefs.

"You just don't know how hard you make me," I said, poking Ashley's thigh again. Ashley jumped off the bed.

"Grow up Ray," Ashley shouted. I smiled at how much the sexual tension made Ashley uncomfortable.

"Be young and dumb Ashley and..." I glanced down as Prince peeked out. "Slob on my knob."

"I'm one of the few women out here who wants to save some things for her husband."

"We're not talking anal or threesomes, Ashley," I explained. "It's just a little head."

"When I have a little husband this won't even be this deep of a discussion. For my husband that's a part of the sex package deal."

"I am your husband," I declared.

"You will be and if you can wait six more months you'll be rewarded," Ashley said as she leaned in to kiss me.

"Damn girl," I said as I stroked Prince. "You drive a hard bargain." I laughed. Ashley did not. She rolled her eyes.

"Stop it,' Ashley whined. "You're acting like a 13-year-old with a newly discovered boner."

"I wish you would embrace it like a horny, curious young lady would...with your mouth," I said with a chuckle. Ashley remained unamused.

"Go to sleep Ray," Ashley said as she rolled over and pulled the fancy duvet cover over her body, tucking herself into a cocoon. I looked over at Ashley not even ten minutes later and she had already fell asleep. I stayed up and watched PornHub on Ashley's smartTV. The conversation Mikey and I had earlier crept back into my mind. *A swim in the sea of plenty would do my body good right now.* I rubbed Ashley's butt as I shrugged my thoughts away and stroked Prince until it went from pimp to a wimp.

Do I really want to marry this girl? How much do I really know about her? Do I really know her at all? "She's good for my future, I reasoned. At 28, Ashley was doing better than most 45-year-olds. I know I caught a good one."

The next morning, I woke up to vindication of my choice in a woman. Ashley, who was already dressed in her royal blue scrubs, cooked my favorite breakfast: French toast, turkey sausage patties and a fried egg over easy, topped with shredded cheddar cheese. She unfolded a breakfast tray over my lap and placed the full plate on it.

"Do you want coffee, apple juice, OJ or water?" She whispered in my ear before kissing my cheek.

"You're too good for me Ashley Jay." Ashley smiled.

"Do you want something to drink, baby?" She asked.

"Coffee please, baby." Ashley returned with a fresh mug, sugar packets and a small silver carafe containing creamer. She looked at her watch and put her hand on her hip. She walked to the closet and pulled out a pair of Crocs. She grabbed her Chanel handbag that was hanging from the doorknob.

"What are your plans for the day?" Ashley asked. "I work until seven tonight. I'm going to Morgan's after that. I'll probably come home to change. Are you working today?" I shook my head no as I stuffed forkfuls in my mouth to refrain from the desire to elaborate.

"But it's Saturday," Ashley pried.

"No. I'm not working today. Unlike you, I don't have to go in everyday."

"Isn't there a party you need to promote or a concert to attend? I know the radio station has some events going on. You don't have to work any of them?" I shook my head no and continued eating. Ashley shrugged and walked toward the bed. She kissed my forehead before she grabbed her car keys off the nightstand.

"We're good, then, baby," I said in between bites. "Have a good day." I smiled until Ashley was out of sight and as soon as I heard the front door close, I hopped out of bed and jumped on the phone.

"I need to meet up with you - like now. Don't ask any questions. I need a big favor. Ok. Bet. You can pick me up from my house in an hour." I got dressed after ending the call. I sent a text to Little Richie to pick me

27

up from Ashley's house. He texted back with the ok and arrived fifteen minutes later.

Forty-five minutes later I hopped into the front seat of a 2017 Toyota Camry. The hot leather seat burned my leg.

"What's the emergency?"

"I need you to help me with something," I said in the most non-emergent way.

"You always want something, King. What do you need that you think I can help with? Me of all people."

"I need your pay stubs," I said.

"My pay stubs? For what?"

"I need your pay stubs because they say Crystal Clear Communications Incorporated on them," I revealed. "I can change your name."

"What type of fraudulent activity are you trying to pull?"

"I don't need a lecture right now, Mikey. I need an answer - preferably a yes."

"You're going to have to give me more than that brother." I knew Mikey would want to know all the details before he'd make a decision.

"I need my girl to believe I still work there," I reasoned.

"But you don't," Mikey countered.

"I need my girl to believe I still work there," I repeated. "Just until the wedding planning is over. I'm sure she'll understand."

"Your fiance, you mean. I think you're going about this all wrong. Why don't you just tell her you lost your job?"

"Again, Mikey, I don't need a lecture. I need your help." I tried to be as sincere as I could to convince Mikey this was something I needed. "It's a matter of life or death, bro. This woman means everything to me. I need her to believe I'm the man I promised her I'd be," I pleaded. I knew playing on Mikey's pro-black love side would prompt him into action.

"I'll see what I can do," Mikey accepted. "We still have to meet for the fitting next week, right," he asked.

"I need like two months worth, before then," I explained. "Like tonight."

"I'll do my best," he said with a heavy sigh.

Taylor
Foolish

"All the things that we accept be the things that we regret..." - Ashanti

I stared at my reflection from the mahogany-framed mirror and twirled as I blasted a *New Edition* mix on my iMusic player. I danced and pranced around my walk-in closet as I searched for something casual to wear for ladies night in.

"You are looking too good," Chris complimented as he walked past me. "Where are you going looking that good?" My husband kissed my neck and grabbed a handful of boob before plopping on the chaise lounge in front of our California king.

"I have to go to Morgan's house," I said with a heavy sigh. "Back to the hood," I added with an eye roll.

"Oh ok. Morgan lives in Federal Hill, right? That's my old neighborhood," Chris said with a nostalgic grin. "I loved it over there."

"Federal Hill," I repeated as I applied lip gloss. "You heard it right the first time...the hood." I pulled my long hair back into a loose ponytail and threw on a fitted dad hat. I wore an HGC Apparel signature 'Black Queen' tank top and tied an oversized, multi-colored flannel shirt around my waist. I slid into a pair of CHANEL thong sandals and pulled matching CHANEL shades from the closet. "I should blend right in with my regular clothes on right? I don't want to get robbed," I said as I blended my MAC clear lipglass with a pink shade and tossed them into my Louis Vuitton makeup bag.

"Taylor, nobody's worried about you. You were once from the hood. You didn't get money like that until middle school, girl, stop it."

"Christopher Morehouse Matthews that is not the point," I shouted out. "Call me bougie if you want but Morgan's house is less than luxurious.

'In fact, I think I saw a rodent the last time I visited. I'm not friends with rodents, insects or any other small creature that by nature are supposed to dwell on the outside of four walls."

"Do not say my government name," Chris interjected. "And not everybody is as financially blessed as your family. Just try to have fun."

"Morehouse, Morehouse, Morehouse," I teased. I grabbed my bag and kissed my husband as I walked out. "I'll try my best."

"I can't stand you," Chris teased back. "Have fun tonight baby. Come home ready for some good loving!"

"I stay ready, baby," I said as I winked and closed the door behind me. I pulled up to Morgan's apartment building, a three-story complex that sat beside a 24-hour laundromat and a pizza takeout restaurant. I looked around reluctant to park my car on her sketchy street. The narrow back alley housed a few homeless guys, who posted up on the corner begging for change and food.

"Of course there's wouldn't be any underground parking or even a decent parking garage," I said as I spotted Ashley's car a few spaces up. "I'm glad she made it here first." I grabbed my signature bottle of Ciroc Red Berry out of the passenger's seat, locked the doors with my alarm key and headed inside.

"Ugh, it smells like a urinal," I realized aloud when I pressed Morgan's apartment number. I hit 308 again until I heard the buzzer unlock the door. I chuckled at the irony of having a locked door to enter a building thieves already live in. Morgan's neighbor had gotten robbed twice in the same week this past month. I knocked on Morgan's door and Ashley answered. We hugged as I walked into Morgan's grand apartment.

"How long have you been here," I asked Ashley.

"For about an hour now," Ashley said. "Morgan's in her room finishing up an interview. You look cute."

31

"Thanks," I said adding a twirl to showcase the entire fashionable 'fit. "You know I had to pull out the sandals. It's barely reaches 75 degrees in April in Providence, girl. I'm basking in the weather. Where's her mom?" I whispered to Ashley after I yelled out hello to Morgan when I walked into the kitchen.

"She's still at the casino. She didn't come back that weekend she and Morgan went away. That's why Morgan pushed Ladies Night back. She had to go back and practically pull her off the blackjack table to bring her mom back."

"Wow, I thought things have gotten better," I said as I pulled a glass from the cabinet and rinsed it out in the sink. "That's sad, you know," I said to Ashley. I opened my bottle of vodka and filled it to the rim. I leaned in and slurped it down then poured a little more.

"Only you, I swear," Ashley said after she entered the kitchen behind me. "Why not pour a more modest amount?"

"Ashley, only you're the modest type. Why not pour a dubious amount and slurp, slurp, slurp,slurp, slurp," I said as I slow-whined and gyrated as if I was in a twerk video. Ashley giggled and joined in on the slow whine to no music. Morgan started to flicker the light switch like a strobe light as she emerged from her bedroom.

"Go. Go. Go," Morgan cheered. She pulled out a bottle of her favorite tequila and poured herself a glass as Ashley and I continued to dance and laugh.

"You have no rhythm whatsoever, Taylor," Morgan observed. "You need some lessons," she stated.

"I was classically trained in jazz and hip-hop," I corrected.

"I can't tell," Morgan said.

"Who crowned you the queen of dance, Laurieann Gibson?" I asked.

"Steve Harvey," Ashley blurted out as she laughed. Ashley poured herself another shot of tequila as she set up the chips on Morgan's coffee table. She shuffled the deck as Morgan and I took our seats. Morgan opted for the dilapidated armchair and I sat next to Ashley on the couch. As the game started, Ashley divulged more about her upcoming nuptials.

"I'm lowkey excited about it," Ashley mentioned for the eleventh time. "I'm going dress shopping soon. The wedding is in seven months." I rolled my eyes as she blabbed about her wedding plans.

"That's good. I'm glad," Morgan said. "I hope you're ready for that feature in the *Gazette*. I know Ray is. He stays camera-ready."

"You'll feature them again? You did a story on the proposal already. And it was announced on Onblast.com," I reminded.

"Stop hating. I'll cover what I want and I want to feature Ashley again," Morgan stated.

"You should be tired of writing the same old stories," I said. "You know, covering something more meaningful than store openings and wedding announcements." Morgan casually dismissed my unsolicited advice with a wave of her hand.

"I am a real journalist that covers stories that mean something to the people who reads them," Morgan retorted. "And *you* love the spotlight. You never seem to mind when the story is about your family. You weren't saying that when I covered you and Chris. You had a full-page spread."

"Correction. We *paid* for a full-page spread. I can't help it if my father invests in his daughter," I said with a shrug of the shoulders. Morgan rolled her eyes again.

"You always go back to the money," Morgan said as she poured another drink.

"Isn't that what you're striving for?" I quipped.

"I work for everything I have. I know working might be a foreign concept to you," Morgan wise-cracked. Ashley lost two games of poker so she had to take another four shots of tequila on top of the four she already had.

"Speaking of work," Ashley chimed in. "Guess who I saw the other day in the ER?" Morgan and I both looked at her anxiously awaiting an answer. "Corrine," Ashley revealed. "And guess what?" Ashley continued after a brief pause. "She's pregnant," she blurted.

"Shut up! Who is she pregnant by? Don't say Travis again?" Morgan asked.

"Yes!" Ashley said in a giddy, drunken voice. "That's exactly who! He was there, too. I turned around as the ambulance pulled up. And boom, there he was; right by her side, holding hands, cradling their baby in his arms."

"Are. You. Serious?" I asked in disbelief. I knew that hurt Ashley considering her history with him. She lost their baby and now he's having another.

"As serious as a heart attack," Ashley as downed another shot of tequila. "He looked nervous. As if he couldn't believe I was the one that would have to save the mother of his child. Err, children."

"What? You had to save her life?" I yelled out, flabbergasted. I almost spit out my drink.

"I had to stabilize her blood pressure so she wouldn't go into premature labor. She's due in five weeks. Travis started to panic when Corrine felt faint so to be on the safe side he brought her to the emergency room. She had preeclampsia."

"Oh my god! What did you say?" Morgan asked. "As much as he runs his mouth about you when I see him. I swear. He never mentioned Corrine having another baby."

"So what happened?" I asked.

"You mean after he cornered me in the hallway outside her hospital room?" Morgan and I nodded in unison. We listened intently like

34

preschoolers during circle time. "I said, 'It looks like another congratulations is in order. You're well on your way to building a little team with Corrine.' He didn't say anything else about it."

"How does that make you feel?" Morgan asked. "Does it drudge up some unresolved feelings?" Morgan sat close to Ashley then laid her head on Ashley's lap.

"Any feelings I had went down the toilet years ago. And seeing them together made it all too real. It was a real reminder that he has the life I wanted with him...with her," Ashley said with an eye roll. "But I guess I'm happy that Travis is happy. Maybe now he can stop harassing my friends with his pledges of his newfound love for me. Especially since he never expresses that when we speak to each other. It's annoying."

"Do you think you're completely over Travis?" I asked an unwavering Ashley Jay.

"I'm not sure if I was ever under Travis to begin with. He let me know where I stood time and time again. And I ignored it because I thought I wanted to be with him. Talk about stuck on stupid!" Ashley exclaimed. "I was just happy someone wanted to have sex with me...considering..."

"Speaking of which...did you tell Ray yet?" I wanted to shift the topic off of Ashley's past man friend onto her more current love affairs.

"No I haven't told Ray anything yet," Ashley said without further explanation. Morgan shook her head in subtle disappointment. I rolled my eyes. "I'm going to, I swear," she added. "I'm sure he's doing just fine without assistance. Emphasis on the ass," Ashley joked, poking her butt out.

"Don't try to laugh away a serious topic," I said.

"No seriously," she said adjusting her posture. "How do you tell someone that?"

"Just remember how you felt when Jay-J did not tell you. Tell Ray what happened. Tell him your side of the story. I'm sure he'll understand."

"You think so?" Ashley asked as hopeful as a poverty-stricken child on Christmas Eve.

"He loves you," I shouted, hoping my tone will get through to Ashley's disbelief.

"You really believe that?" Ashley asked. Morgan and I were both in agreeance - a rarity. "I'm not convinced the black Hugh Hefner reincarnate is all of a sudden ready to settle down.

"I'll tell him when I think he's ready for real about his future with me. That's not something everybody should know anyway. It gives the wrong people ammunition for betrayal."

"You're overthinking it," I said. "Just tell him. If he accepts that, then great. Go off and get married and have some more babies and enjoy your life."

"And if he doesn't?" Ashley asked. Before anyone could answer, Ashley continued. "I'm just not convinced Ray is any different than Travis or Jay-J, for that matter. Most men are opportunists for the cooch. This whole engagement may be the charade of his life."

"What would convince you that he is actually different?" Morgan asked.

"The truth," Ashley said cryptically. "I get this funny feeling that Ray tells me anything, as if I'm so gullible and naive. If I learned anything from that Jay-J experience is to trust my intuition instead of doubt it. And I'm not sure about Ray."

"Could it be that you're just paranoid because of what you been through? Not all men are the same," I reminded. "Look at Chris. He's used to run through chicks."

'Which is the exact reason why you're so adamant that he's cheating on you now, isn't it?" Morgan asked.

"Girl, if you don't," I muttered to Morgan through clenched teeth. "Can't you see I'm trying to give the girl some hope?"

"Don't be foolish, woman, if you're not fully convinced that he has changed, then he probably hasn't."

"Whatever," I said. "Thanks for the advice. How long have you been married? Or in a relationship? Oh okay then."

"I'm married to God. I have a relationship with my damn self and my career is blossoming. And guess who's not stressed out and broke?" Morgan asked sarcastically as she raised her hand in the air and waved it back and forth.

"I'm not nor will I ever be stressed or broke over some grown ass boy."

"Morgan, be real...you wish you had a man. No man doesn't equate to no worries. It's just you worry about different things."

"Yeah, and none of them are 'I wonder if my man is cheating.' I'm not that foolish. No woman should be."

"You two are wearing out my peacemaking skills," Ashley said in a tipsy slur. "You both are being childish and my story was interrupted. It was good too." Ashley rambled on as she took another shot. "Can I finish my Travis story now?"

"Go ahead, girl, get it off your chest," Morgan said.

"Yes finish up and move on!" I said with a side eye.

"I fell more love into the idea of us. What I wanted from anyone who wanted to give it to me - a something real. And that was something Travis never planned on giving me.

"What about the baby?" I asked. "How do you feel about him having another baby?"

"What about it?" Ashley quipped. "I don't feel any type of way about it. I told you if he likes it...I love it."

"I'm not convinced. I don't believe you," Morgan followed up. "That was real between you and Travis."

"I don't think so. Real is mutual. Real is reciprocal. A one-sided relationship is not real. What's real is that it's really over with Travis," Ashley said with a shrug. "I did end that night pulling some plastic apparatus off a guy's penis. You gotta love the ER!" Ashley poured more tequila in her shot glass. She held the neck of the bottle, paused for a moment then sighed and took another shot.

"It's baby season, everywhere," Morgan said. "Because I swear the photography intern they paired me with is pregnant. There must be something in the water."

"Good thing I think water is disgusting," Ashley said. "I don't want anymore babies."

"I want another one," I said. "Chris doesn't. We can't afford it," I mocked. "Speaking of not being able to afford stuff," I said with a mean girl grin. "How's work, Morgan?" Ashley shook her head in disappointment.

"Funny," Morgan responded. "Work is ok. People are going crazy over the latest round of layoffs. But they got me working on another fashion piece. I told my editor I'm tired of doing these fluff stories. I told her I'm ready to hold big business accountable, expose government scandal and cover more interesting stories than Jaxon's latest commercial real estate investment or the opening of a new store."

"So how did that conversation go?" Ashley asked tentatively.

"She took it as me wanting more responsibility," Morgan sighed. "So, now I'm paired with this new girl, a photography intern. I can't remember her name, Alicia, Alissa or Alaia something. But I'm in charge of showing her how to be a better storyteller through her snapshots. She works nights as waitress at Harry's and goes to school during the day," Morgan said with a hint of judgment.

"She hopes to be an editorial photographer when she graduates later this summer. She does shoots for weddings and corporate events as a freelancer. But, I digress. I'm not a babysitter but apparently..."

"You are," I said with a laugh as I finished Morgan's sentence.

"That's what's up," Ashley said.

"No, it's not really. She has to be like five or six months pregnant, easy," Morgan said. "Besides the fact that she has had a little gut since she started, she keeps like hinting towards it. She says things like, 'babies are such a blessing - not matter how they got here.' Nobody says stuff like that unless she's in a messy situation. Maybe she doesn't know who her kid's father is," Morgan affirmed. "Maybe it's because of work. Most people don't tell that information off hand."

"Maybe she's just a private person and wants to keep things under wraps," Ashley said. "It could be because she just started her internship. Some things need to be private, you know just in case they decide to let her go, too."

"Not everyone is as private as you are," I pointed out.

"It's weird," Morgan noted. "I know she's pregnant. I just know. The dude might be married or something." We all laughed because Morgan was eerily clairvoyant, often foreseeing future events and knowing details before anyone tells her.

"I would kill somebody if Chris was out here with a baby," I said with a sly grin. "He already knows that!"

"Why would you even think that?" Ashley asked. "Chris is the most devoted family man I've ever seen."

"Well, best friend, you might need your eyes checked. Chris isn't the knight in shining armour he portrays himself to be. At least, not lately. He's never home. And blames it on my extravagant spending habits..."

I said with a shrug of the shoulders. "Even though I'm spending with credit cards my father has always paid. So I smell bullshit," I said nonchalantly as I called Chris to check on Kaila and he didn't answer. "See. Mr. Devoted is never available."

"Maybe he's asleep since he works so much. Don't jump to conclusions, Taylor. You used to like the fact that he worked so much," Ashley pointed out.

"Yes, " Morgan said as she rolled her eyes back to the white. "I remember how you used to say it loud and proud, 'My man is going to be a firefighter; he's going to be an EMT.' You bragged all the time," Morgan added.

"I liked his drive, yes," I corrected. "I also liked how much time he made for me *in spite* of how much he worked. I don't get that Chris anymore. The Chris I get now complains about how much money I spend, criticizes how I choose to spoil our daughter and hassles me to be the wife he signed up for. You know cook, clean and come...I miss the old Chris," I concluded as I received an alert from my phone.

"A message from Mama Matthews," I muttered. "Come and get your daughter by midnight or she's spending the night," I read aloud. I looked at my phone in disbelief and dialed Chris's cell phone number again. This time it went straight to his voicemail, which sparked a bigger fire on the inside of me. I re-dialed his number and got the same response.

"What's going on Taylor," Ashley asked.

"I just got this weird text. I'm trying to reach Chris but there's no answer," I said. Morgan drunkenly chuckled. I shot at stern look her way and she quickly apologized. I looked toward the ceiling, closed my eyes and sighed before dialing my mother-in-law's number.

"Hey, Mama Matthews. How are you doing tonight? I just got your message. Is everything ok?" I asked, perplexed and concerned at the same time. Chris's mother never reached out to me directly. She only calls Chris.

"I'm doing fine. I'll do much better when you come get your daughter," Mama Matthews huffed. She was a far from an old-school grandma who liked to spend time with her grands. She was this new-age 'glam-ma' who reserved her weekends for nights at random jazz spots, hoping to go home with the drummer of the band.

"My daughter? How did she end up in Warwick? I left her in her pajamas with her father. Where is Chris?"

"That's something you're going to have to ask him," Mama Matthews said.

"Mama, she can't stay the night. She has an early playdate on our side of town. And I'm not home. Where is Chris? I've had these plans for weeks. Where did he go?" Mama Matthews remained silent. She never told me anything when it came to Chris. She was his vault of secrets.

"What time will you get here?" Mama Matthews asked, ignoring all of my questions. "You know Warwick is a long drive from Federal Hill. Have you been drinking?"

"Chris told you where I was but you can't tell me where he is?" I asked peeved. "It will be longer for me to drive from your house to mine."

"What time will you get here," Mama Matthews repeated.

"I'll be there by midnight," I said with a heavy sigh. I hung up and checked the time was 11:15 p.m. I rolled my eyes and walked into the kitchen to brew some coffee. "You don't have Starbucks coffee?" I asked, sighing in disappointment, already aware of the answer. "Of course you don't."

"Only bougie girls buy Starbucks," Morgan yelled from the living room. I rolled my eyes and scooped the Folgers into the filter. I drank two cups of hot, black coffee to sober up quick. I grabbed a 10-ounce bottle of water out the fridge to take with me on the twenty minute ride.

"I thought you said your landlord replaced those with French doors," I pointed out.

"No, I said my new doors open like French doors," Morgan reminded.

"Oh. I was about to tell you that your landlord lied, honey!" I laughed. "Those are the same cheap doors Chris tried to convince me to get when we redid our walk-in closet," I said. Morgan stared darts at Ashley who chimed in seconds later.

"Don't be like that Taylor," Ashley said. "Not everyone can go home to luxury."

"She don't even go home to luxury," Morgan said with a laugh. "You're not fooling anyone, with your fake designer shades and borrowed handbags. You can't even afford your house. That's why Chris works so hard. You're no better than the rest of us, homie."

"Not better? I own a half-a-million dollar home in Riverside, girl, please. And act like you don't know that my father runs the real estate game in Providence."

"You just got a rich daddy, girl. But what do you do?" Morgan asked with a smirk.

"You know what your problem is? You wish your man was your daddy. Poor Chris. Does he know he'll never live up to your expectations?" Morgan said in a baby voice as she pouted her lips.

"Funny, you sound just like your drunk mother. Where is she? Spending your hard-earned money on booze and bar bets. Or is she spending her weekend with the latest dirty old man. What will that be stepdaddy number five?"

"That's enough ladies, damn," Ashley refereed. "You both need to chill. Hitting below the belt ain't never been cool. And we are not those kind if friends."

I stood up with my hands folded, glaring at Morgan. She had her feet dangling off the side of her armchair as she stared out the window.

'No, Ashley Jay. Let Morgan get whatever she has in her heart off her chest. I'm so sick of the subliminals."

"You only respond to subliminal shit," Morgan said as she threw her hands up. She talked with her hands whenever she started feeling the spirits. "I honestly don't think you can handle my directness. It intimidates you."

"Please. I wish I would be scared of you," I said.

"You're only saying anything because you're juiced. You must still have some Ciroc in your system because you're too powered up right now," Morgan countered. "You wouldn't be this tough. You're not this tough."

"Please," Ashley said. "I can't take this arguing. It's so childish."

"No, Ashley Jay, let her say what it is she *really* wants to say. I want to know how she *really* feels about me," I insisted.

"You're a brat," Morgan blurted out. "There, I said it!"

"And you're poor," I countered.

"There's a big difference between working for what you have and striving to accomplish your goals," Ashley scolded.

"And that's not you're doing," Morgan added. "Using your man for his status. Spending all his hard-working earnings for your trivial pursuits and neglecting your daughter. Should I keep going?"

"Please," I insisted as I gathered my things. I slid into my thong sandals and tossed my shades into my handbag.

"You're not a good friend. Hell, you're barely a good person. You hide behind your material things hoping they hide your bitterness. You hope your things shine for you but Taylor Smith Matthews is nothing more than a selfish, spoiled brat with mommy issues." Morgan laughed and finished the last of her drink. I took a deep breath and grabbed my half-full bottle of Ciroc off the kitchen counter.

43

"Morgan that was so uncalled for," Ashley said breaking moments of awkward silence.

"Taylor asked for it," Morgan said.

"No, she's right. I asked for it but not this," I said as I pointed around. "Your hellhole you call an apartment is making me itch. I think I got hives from your sofa. My Chanel bag isn't accustomed to this level of filth."

"Ashley Jay, get your friend," Morgan replied as Ashley moved closer to me. She stood in between me and Morgan like a protective barrier.

"Ashley's friend is leaving," I said as I threw my bag over my shoulder. "Ashley hit me up when you're in better company." I air kissed in Ashley's direction as I walked to the door. "Bye," I snarled at Morgan as I left. I got in the truck and dialed Chris's number again before I pulled off. Still no answer. *What could he be doing?* I wondered as I dialed the number to the fire station.

"Chris isn't on the schedule," the operator said after I asked to speak to him.

"I know. He's supposed to be off until Sunday so he must have been called in tonight. Maybe around nine or so," I responded.

"We do not have any record of Chris being on-call this week. And he's not on the log for tonight either. The only thing I have him on schedule for is his regular shift, which starts Sunday, like you said," the operator explained.

"Ok. Thank you," I said, hanging up the phone. I pulled up to Mama Matthew's house. It was pitch black. I knocked on the door. I looked inside the window of the door. I banged the door. One light turned on then the door opened.

"You're late," Mama Matthews said as she guided me inside.

44

"I'm early. It's 11:59. Where's Kaila?"

"In her pajamas in my bed," Mama snarked.

"I just drove from downtown and I have another 15-minute drive home. Can you please just go get my daughter?" I said, nearing defeat. Mama Matthews flicked on the kitchen light. Kaila rocked back and forth in her car seat, fully-dressed and asleep. "Did Chris mention where he was going or the reason he would drop her off to you without calling me?"

"I asked him the same thing," she said as she handed me Kaila's bag and blanket. "Chris said he wanted to give you some alone time because you've been bitchy lately," Mama revealed, adding an eye roll. The secrets Mama Matthews managed to tell always had something to do with a behavior of mine that either she or Chris felt needed correction.

"Ok. Thank you for keeping her," I said as I hoisted Kaila's car seat off the table.

"You're welcome," she mumbled before slamming the door. I secured Kaila into the backseat and got into the driver's seat. I called Chris again. It went straight to voicemail. I shook my head, holding back tears and fighting my negative thoughts. Chris only acted funny with me when it came to one other woman - his mama and he wasn't at her house. I drove home. When I got in the house, Chris was sitting on the sofa, flipping through cable channels.

"My girls are home," Chris exclaimed as he held his arms out for a hug.

"Where were you?" I asked as I handed him his daughter.

"I had to go in," Chris said as he carefully took Kaila out of her car seat.

"To work?" I asked.

"Yes," Chris said. He smiled after he kissed his sleeping beauty. He took her jacket off. I handed him her pajamas from her diaper bag. Chris changed Kaila's clothes and put her in her bedroom.

"Because I thought it was odd that you didn't tell me and then you were unreachable," I said as I began to take my shoes off.

"Since when do you not trust me?" Chris asked with a smirk. He reached out to grab my foot and began to massage it.

"Since the very beginning. Since Austynn. Since Amera. Since Amber. You got a thing for chicks with A names. I'm surprised you didn't give Ashley a shot."

"Where is all this coming from?"

"I know that you're hiding something. Why did you drop off Kaila with your mom instead of calling me to get her?"

"What's up with this random argument? I wanted you to have some time to yourself since you've been so..."

"Bitchy lately?" I asked. "Isn't that what you said to your mom?"

"How was your night out?" Chris asked ignoring my suspicions.

"Where were you?" I repeated.

"I already told you," Chris snapped. "Now if you're done with this interrogation, I'd like to watch a movie with my wife."

"I'm not totally convinced you were at work," I said.

"My paycheck will reflect the extra time. When you have extra spending money, you'll know I am not lying to you."

"So you went to work without telling me to get extra spending money for me? Even though your biggest problem is me spending your hard-earned money?"

"Yes, girl, now get over her and love on your man," Chris said as he pulled me closer to him. "I just want to provide for you the way you're used to...better even."

"Well why do you have to be so secretive to do it?"

46

"I'm not hiding anything from you girl...it's your paranoia."

"Or it's my woman's intuition," I responded, still not convinced I was getting the whole story from my husband but I digress. I had my own plan to get my husband and I back on the same page. It would take a little time, but it will reveal whatever he's hiding.

Chris
Confessions
"Trying to figure it out how I'm going to let this come out of my mouth..." - Usher

I reached out to Taylor as she reluctantly moved closer to me. I brushed away loose hairs from around her face and pulled her into a kiss. Taylor smelled like passionfruit and her plump lips tasted like cupcakes.

"Why don't you change? Get comfortable and tell me about your night," I whispered in her ear. Ten minutes later Taylor re-emerged from our bedroom in a see-through negligee. "Tell Daddy about your night."

"I'd rather you talk to my southern lips and help me forget," Taylor hinted.

"That bad, huh?" She nodded and bit her bottom lip, which immediately turned me on. I obliged to her request and caressed her skin softly with the tips of my fingers. I kissed her body slowly from her neck to her feet. Taylor moaned in anticipation as I sucked toe by toe and kissed up her legs to her inner thigh. I slid her panties over and planted my tongue on her exposed clitoris. I swirled my tongue around until her pussy gushed. I sucked her clit and fingered her at the same time. Minutes later Taylor burst her lady juices all over my face. She stood up to return the favor, with shaking legs and all. While she was asleep I heard a faint noise coming from the bathroom.

I leaped out the bed to retrieve the hidden device and stop it from vibrating again before it awakened light-sleeping Taylor. I grabbed the phone from atop of the medicine cabinet. I flipped the device open and read a text message from an old friend.

"We need to talk it's urgent," the message read.

"Where would you want to meet?" I texted.

'At a public spot with plenty of witnesses - but private enough to discuss us."

'Us. You know I'm married," I replied.

"I know. I don't care about that," the text said.

"Well...I do. You can't just jump back into my life because you're divorced now."

"This is one of the reasons for the divorce."

"How? You've been married for the last seven years. I got married nearly four years ago. We haven't been in contact since, well...you know what happened."

"Since Keith. I know. But this isn't about Keith, it's about Kristian."

"What does your son have to do with any of this?" I replied.

"Just meet me at Bar Louie's," the text said. I simply replied ok and went back into my bedroom. I looked over at a sleeping Taylor as I threw on some gray sweatpants, a white t-shirt and a black hoodie. I gave her a kiss on the cheek and stepped out.

I pulled up to the eatery, hesitant to go inside. I was actually surprised that she reached out and enthralled at what she could possibly have to tell me since it had been a while since we spoke, let alone seen each other face to face. I walked in and sat at the crowded bar. A flamboyant bartender sauntered over to me.

"What you drinking tonight, handsome?" He leaned in to hear my order.

"Whiskey. Straight up."

"Well. Ok. Something strong for a strong man," he said as he leaned back. "I'm Brian. I'll be your server," he said with a wink before scribbling in his black notepad. He pulled a bottle from the top shelf behind the bar and poured me a glass. He slid the glass across the bartop and I caught it. "You're on point tonight, I see." Brian laughed and switched back to me with a receipt. I slid him my bank card. "Hold it, brother, start a tab," I said. I took a sip of the drink and felt a rub across my shoulder.

"I'm glad I could pry you away from your family life on such short notice," a familiar voice spoke softly, close to my ear.

"Austynn Richards," I said with a slight smile. "Nice to see you. I needed a drink so it was nothing to drive out here."

"It's back to Lewis actually and thanks for coming. Let's get right to it, shall we?" Austynn said as she shuffled through her large Michael Kors handbag. She pulled out a legal-sized envelope. "I wanted to show you my divorce papers." I gulped the rest of my drink and motioned for Brian to return.

"Another one? He asked. I nodded and he poured. This time he handed the drink to me. "Would you like something?" I asked Austynn. She declined.

"So you're divorce is final," I said as I inspected the papers she handed to me. "How is this relevant to me?" I asked as I handed her divorce decree back to her.

"You didn't read the part where Keith asked for a paternity test?" Austynn asked.

"I did but again, not to be rude, but what does this have to do with me?"

"Keith had his reservations about Kristian."

"How does this concern me?" I asked again. I grew more agitated whenever she mentioned his name.

"Well, if you would allow me elaborate... I nodded for her to proceed. "My entire pregnancy Keith insisted on getting a paternity test but I declined because I assured him I knew he was the father. 'I didn't mix up my dates.' I would tell him because I knew you and I weren't reckless when we messed around on the low."

"I know. Usually we were careful. But there was that drunk night in NYC that October before you had Kristian?"

"I remember that night. The details are vague but I remember condoms being all over the room the next morning."

"Yeah, the details are fuzzy but I don't remember seeing any open wrappers or used condoms either. That's the night that made me question you about everything when I found out you were pregnant. But what did you tell me ten?"

"The same thing I told Keith. I don't mix up my dates. I know who I had sex with and that's honestly what I thought. My adamant stance appeased him for a little while. But it was like Keith kept Kristian under a microscope as if Keith was trying to discover where his own genealogy was in his so-called offspring. His consistency to search didn't lead him anywhere. Any similarities Keith found made him point out differences about Kristian that I couldn't explain off."

"Like what?"

"Like he has your cheekbones. His hands and feet are shaped like yours. Kristian has a runner's body build and the way he sleeps with his legs cocked open. It broke Keith that he couldn't find any solid proof by physical resemblance that Kristian was his son. Keith lived in the past and picked apart every detail of his memory. And all it did was point to you."

"Me? I had nothing to do with your relationship after you chose that clown over me."

"You know how close we were before I married Keith. Everyone did. They could see our connection and Keith was far from blind. Even though we weren't in contact, when I defended myself against Keith's asinine accusations of you being Kristian's father, it made things worse. You were a constant thorn in Keith's side that he nursed with tequila." I tried to hide my delight that I had an affect on Keith like that. I smiled slyly as I sipped the smooth cognac while Austynn continued with her story.

"His random drinking became habitual. He started leaving us for days at a time. At first it would be a Tuesday night. Then he spent weekends away. When he returned, he was either too hungover to function and bedridden for hours, unable to stand upright, stumbling drunk and argumentative," she reminisced. Austynn paused and looked at me. Her sullen stare into my eyes reminded me of how she looked at me in the past, like she needed a savior.

"It was like Keith was looking for a reason to build a wedge between him and I. Things got really bad when he lost his job. It was right around the time Kristian fell in love with firefighters, which fueled Keith's hatred toward you even more. Keith went into a deep depression and wasn't quite right afterwards. That's when he drank even more heavily, argued whenever we spoke and accused me of everything from sleeping with married men to selling my stuff on the corner.

He turned into a totally different person and..."Austynn sighed and put her head down to disguise the tears welling in her eyes.

"Again, I'm still not hearing the relevance to me?" I said visibly upset that Keith still affected her in that way. "Why are you spilling the details of the demise of your marriage to someone who warned you against marrying him?"

"I'm getting there - bear with me. I asked for a legal separation when he started treating Kristian with disdain during his drunken rants. The courts granted the separation and out of spite, Keith filed for divorce."

"I'm sorry to hear that," I said, even though I wasn't.

"I'm not. My son needed a stable, loving environment and that wasn't what we gave him. Those elements were lost in our home. During the divorce proceedings, Keith asked for a paternity test and the pending results would determine the outcome of the divorce. If Keith was Kristian's father then he would work on the marriage by going to counseling. But if he was not the father, then Keith would proceed with the divorce." She slid a mailing envelope with legal documents inside across the table to me again.

"Read it again," she said as she pulled out the test results. "Keith was 99.9% out of the running." The paper said Keith had zero percent chance of being Kristian's father. I looked up from the paper and summoned the waiter again.

"I'm going to need something stronger," I told him. "Let me get a double shot of whiskey." I refocused on Austynn. My heart jumped, stopped then doubled its speed. "So what does this mean?"

"It means there's a congratulations in order for you," Austynn half-joked. "You are the only other option," Austynn murmured. The waiter returned with my drink. He placed the napkin on the table then reached for the full glass on his tray. I snatched it before he could and gulped it before he noticed. The shocked waiter reached for the empty glass. "Another one. Stat. Please. Thank you," I said as he rolled his eyes and left to retrieve my order.

"I hate to spring this on you like this. I felt this was something too important to wait," Austynn said. I sat in disbelief at the thought that I fathered my firstborn almost four years before I had my firstborn.

"But I asked you if there was any possibility damn near seven years ago. You swore there was no chance I could be that kid's father. Now the kid is 6 and you want me to believe you that I am in fact Kristian's father just because Keith isn't."

"It's the truth, Chris. And you know it," Austynn said. I finished my third round, took a $50 bill from my wallet and dropped it on the table. "You can take a test, too, if that will make you feel better," Austynn said as I stepped back from the table. "But we both know he's yours." I looked at my watch and sighed.

"It's late. I need to get home. I'll be in touch," I said as I inched closer toward the exit.

"Chris...don't leave like this. Let's talk about it," Austynn pleaded. Austynn looked up at me with puppy dog eyes. She grabbed my hand and held it momentarily before I snatched it away quickly.

"No. I need to go. It's too much to wrap my head around. Talking about it won't help or change the past. I need time to think about what I'm going to do," I revealed.

"Ok. Well don't take too long. Kristian needs his father. Keith dropped him like a dead rat the moment he got those results," Austynn said. I chuckled slightly. *And that's the man you chose*, I evilly thought.

53

"I have a family to get home to Austynn. I think you have a child to get home to, so, goodnight," I said. I looked back at Austynn as I left the bar. She looked over the papers, returned them to her handbag and sat silently with her hands folded under her chin. The waiter returned and Austynn handed him the money I left on the table. I heard him ask where I went and Austynn said he left and pointed to the door as I practically ran to my car. I jumped on the freeway and drove around the city until I pulled up into the driveway of my home and stumbled inside.

Taylor was still asleep when I snuck back in the house. I hopped in the shower before getting into bed. I climbed into my King-sized bed and wrapped myself in our Egyptian cotton duvet. I laid next to her as the room spun around with my thoughts traveling just as fast.

How dare Austynn drop this bomb on me about Kristian? How do I know if she is even telling the truth? Austynn was the person I always had a thing for - regardless of we had going on with other people. There were no titles yet our connection was more than physical.

It was a meeting of the minds and a meshing of the souls. Somewhere along the line, my heart became intertwined while she became insatiable. Then all of a sudden Austynn was in a relationship with Keith. But that wasn't the end; we still had a connection. She always talked about what-ifs but never tried to go all the way. I always felt that I was never good enough for her. Then she got married on a brother. I sighed at the memory.

When Austynn married Keith, I was devastated. I told myself I was happy for her until I believed it. I convinced myself this was for the best. At least I still had Taylor. Taylor has been my ride-or-die through all the randoms, flings and hookups that I had used to cope after Austynn's rejection, which ultimately caused drama between Taylor and I.

I looked at Taylor. I gave her cheek a gentle kiss. *She loves me.* And I love her for how hard she loves for me. I pulled her into a tight hug. *I hope this next ride isn't too bumpy for her.* I tried to think of how to tell her about Kristian and shook off the feelings of regret as I watched Taylor breathe. *She looks so peaceful.* I sighed heavily. I knew that once she found out about the possibility that Kristian is mine Taylor would cause World War III quicker than Trump. *I have to hold off on telling her, but juggling both is going to be difficult.*

Taylor's jealous mindset won't be able to handle there being another woman with my child, especially not Austynn. *I may have a son.* A sense of pride and responsibility came over me with the thought. *I have to be in his life. I have to be the kind of father I didn't have. Regardless of how Taylor may feel about it.* I turned over to try to sleep off my helluva night.

The next morning I woke up to a hot breakfast: sweet grits, two slices of rye toast, a fried egg and three strips of turkey bacon. Taylor sat at the breakfast bar as she flipped through the pages of *Essence* Magazine. She poured a glass of Pellegrino water then sipped the remainder from the bottle.

"I'm going in early today," I broke it to Taylor as she poured me a glass of orange juice.

"Ugh, Chris, really?" She answered just as I expected her to. Taylor looked at the wall clock. "I take it you didn't read my note?"

"Really," I responded as I ate. "Just know I'm doing this for us. What note?"

"The one I put with your food," she said as she pointed to the table. A letter on our monogram stationery from our wedding. I grabbed the note and read it out loud.

> I miss my husband. The one who made time for me throughout his day to remind me that I was his and he was mine. The guy who sent me flowers; who would text me every hour. The one who would only leave me to save someone's life... Where did that man go?

I put the note back on the table. "I'm still here. I'm just busy, you know rebuilding our savings, paying off that $500,000 mortgage and a Benz note and your Acura truck all while you do what you do best - shop."

"You love saying that, but my father still pays my credit cards and my car, which is almost paid off...so try again."

"Here we go," I said as I walked into the bathroom. I locked the door and ran the shower water. I reached above the medicine cabinet and grabbed the small cell phone from the top shelf. I sat on the toilet and went through the call log and text messages.

"Your excuses are getting old," Taylor shouted from behind the closed door. "I got married to have a husband - not a workaholic. It's not even 8 o'clock yet." Taylor yelled out. "And you came in late last night. Did you get called in again?"

"You know I'm always on call," I said as I put the phone back in my hiding spot. I unlocked the door and cracked it ajar."I...I'm just trying to live up to the promise I gave you - and your dad. I made sure he knew I would take care of you and Kaila as he would. At least I'm not asking him for a loan."

"I think I have a solution," Taylor said. Moments later Taylor pulled the shower curtain back. "I'm going to go back to work."

"Go back? Babe, first, you kind of need to have a job to go back to," I said after a brief chuckle. Taylor rolled her eyes but continued with excitement.

"You know what I mean - I'm going to start working again," Taylor replied. "And all I have to do is call Daddy. He'll be happy to put me to work."

"Some people aren't as lucky as you. Not everyone can just call their dad today and start a job - earning a six-figure salary, at that."

"You think Daddy will pay me that much?" Taylor asked with a Grinch grin. "It's not like I'm walking into a corner office or anything."

"You'll be damn near close. I'm sure he'll make you his brand manager or business partner," I said with a laugh. "You'll make up a title and Mr. Jaxon would allow it. Nepotism at its finest."

I got out the shower and stood on the mat as Taylor patted my body dry with a towel. She wrapped the towel around my waist. I walked into our bedroom and my uniform was laid across the bed. My boxer shorts were always neatly pressed. They were still warm when I slid them on. Taylor sat on the side of the bed and watched me as I did my after-shower routine.

"Be that as it may, I'll still be working. My dad won't give me an easy ride. I'll be better off working for Miss Amy's catering business. I just don't want to do deliveries or party set-ups. It's like I'm the help."

"You will definitely need to be knee-deep in paperwork with your kind of attitude. Customer service is not your strong suit," I noted.

"What is that supposed to mean? You don't know how I am at work. I have great customer service skills." Taylor was offended but I was not lying. "You sound like Morgan," she added with a pout.

"You never did tell me what happened last night," I reminded her. She rolled her eyes as Kaila interrupted. Her curly fro was ill-shaped from bed head. She had one sock on and her pajama dress of Disney's black princess was crooked.

"Good morning beautiful," I said as I walked toward my daughter. She wiped her eyes with a balled fist. "Do you want Daddy to make you some of his famous pancakes?" Kaila's eyes widened and she nodded in excitement. "Go brush your teeth and then have a seat at the table big girl." I kissed her and guided her to the bathroom. Taylor followed and helped Kaila as I started her breakfast.

"Breakfast is ready," I said to Kaila as I placed her Princess plate in front of her. Minnie Mouse-shaped pancakes with strawberry earrings and whipped cream eyes made Kaila's morning every time. I let Kaila pour her own syrup and she drowned Minnie. She used her plastic fork to swirl the whipped cream eyes before digging in.

She dragged the pancake to her mouth, spilling a puddle of sticky sweetness on the mahogany wood table. Taylor sighed and ran into the kitchen to grab a wet rag.

"Daddy will see you later Princess," I said as I kissed Kaila goodbye. "Have fun with Mommy today. I'll see you later."

"How convenient that you're leaving and you left a mess for me to clean."

"I had to give you something to do," I said as I gave Taylor a kiss. "You know you gotta earn that spending money, girl." I slapped Taylor's booty and kissed her again.

"I thought I earned it last night," she countered. "Have a good day at work baby. We'll see you...later?"

"Yes, later. I should be home for dinner," I said. I walked to the front door then turned quickly around and ran past Taylor, who brought Kaila's plate into the kitchen.

"What did you forget?" Taylor asked from the kitchen sink.

"Deodorant," I said as I ran past her, tucking my second cell phone into a side pocket. "I'll see you later." I headed off to work.

After a long shift of answering non-emergent calls of trapped cats, drunken brawls gone wrong and drop-offs at the hospital, I drove home dreading the atmosphere. Right before I turned onto Riverside Drive, I received a text message from Austynn. It was a picture of Kristian in fireman pajamas.

"He's ready for his sleepover," the message captioned.

"Where is he off to?" I replied.

"A friend's house from camp," Austynn answered. "He's staying over until tomorrow. He's going to camp from there and returning in the afternoon."

"Oh, sounds like fun. Tell him I said to behave and enjoy. And when do you think we could meet up?" I replied.

"Meet up?" Austynn replied back.

"I want to buy one of those at-home paternity tests. I'm just trying to do the right thing," I replied. "It can be whenever you're free. I'll clear up my schedule."

"When do you want to do it? Kristian has a dentist appointment next week. Wednesday. We can meet up then."

"Ok. Sounds good. Enjoy your night."

"You too," I said.

"I will," she said. I smiled then turned the phone off. I tucked it in the glove compartment underneath some papers and opened the garage. I walked into the house and called out for my wife. No answer. I called out my daughter's name. No answer. I walked through the house and called out again. I followed the trail of clothes left of the floor that lead to the back door. I walked through the glass door to the back deck. Taylor was half naked in the jacuzzi drinking a glass of Ciroc.

"Where's Kaila?" I asked, sipping from the glass Taylor offered when she saw me.

"At the Blackstone with Daddy," Taylor replied. "Miss Amy wanted to keep her and you know Dad couldn't resist an extra day with his only granddaughter."

"That's nice. I see you're enjoying your quiet time," I said as I lifted the bottle of wine.

"I only agreed to Kaila sleeping over so we can have some alone time," Taylor hinted. I grabbed a glass from the behind the mini bar next to the jacuzzi. I began to undress and hoped in the steamy water next to my beautiful wife.

"Guess what," she said, enthusiastically. "You're looking at the newest human resource manager of S. M. Commercial Realty. I took over hiring for all three of Daddy's locations."

"Cheers to you, baby," I said as our glasses clinked together. I kissed Taylor's cheek.

"Thank you," Taylor said. She took a gulf and put her glass to the side. "It feels good to prove them wrong."

"Who?"

"Morgan," Taylor revealed. "She thinks I'm using you to emulate my relationship with my dad. Morgan believes you work so hard because I'm spoiled and you're trying to live up to these high expectations I have."

"You don't have to prove anything to anyone," I reassured my wife. Taylor was always the type to make a point when people discredit her capabilities. People tend to underestimate Taylor.

"I am my father's child you know? I have a hustler's spirit that came straight from him. I'm more ambitious than I'm given credit for, despite the fact that I don't have to be."

"You're a Daddy's girl who can get whatever she asks for. A lot of people won't understand that. It's rare."

"I asked for a job. Not a milli or a trust fund advance."

"That fact that you have a trust fund and could actually finesse a cool mill from your pops is probably her point," I admitted.

"Oh, so you think I'm a spoiled brat, too?" Taylor asked as if she was offended knowing her bougie attitude. I belted out a slight chuckle then cleared my throat when Taylor shot a stern look of disapproval.

"Morgan called you spoiled?" I asked, not entirely surprised. Morgan had the opposite relationship with her father than Taylor has with Mr. Jax. Morgan has always had to work to survive. Taylor couldn't relate; she had the privileges a wealth of money provided since she was ten.

"Yes," Taylor affirmed. "And Ashley didn't defend me, which speaks volumes." She paused. "Oh and apparently I'm a bad mother," she added. My silence did not appease her.

"I wouldn't say bad at all. Why would she call you a bad mother? I would call you a new-age mom," I said.

"What does that mean?" Taylor said huffy.

"It means you're more carefree. There's no real structure to your routine. You don't have those old-school roots like my mom," I mentioned as Taylor rolled her eyes. "Well like Ashley then."

"Ashley?" Taylor repeated, confused. "What in the world do you mean?"

'Ashley has Isaiah on a set schedule. She fed him homemade baby food when he was younger. He eats salads and tried asparagus. Like, now many 6-year-olds do you know that eats *and likes* vegetables? She reads to him. And now he reads to her. It's impressive."

"Well, Kaila is half his age. She's *only* three," Taylor snarked. "Of course she doesn't know how to read yet. And she's a toddler so she eats like one; picky and random. That doesn't make me a bad mom because I feed her what she likes to eat."

"I know, baby. But McDonald's is not what I would call a healthy meal three times a week because Kaila won't eat your dinner preferences of lobster rolls and caviar."

"So you agree with them?" Taylor asked sullenly.

"I'm not saying that you're a bad mom. You make sure Kaila eats and she's clean. You do put a heavy focus on fashion and appearance. Kaila's room is hooked up. She has the latest gadgets and toys. And Kaila stays fly. But her reading readiness and her food habits comes from Miss Amy taking the time with her going over flashcards and feeding her that good food."

"Miss Amy is a caterer. She has an upper hand in the food department," Taylor pointed out. "And she only has her no more than twice a week. So it's easier for Kaila to do that stuff for fun with her," she reasoned. "With me she doesn't let up. She'll whine and throw a tantrum, screaming and hollering. Who wants to deal with that every time she has to eat?"

"You've got to admit that your patience is thin when it comes to that level of parenting," I said.

"So you're basically cosigning with them? Leave this alone. Please. Let's just end this conversation right here, right now," Taylor said sternly as she exited the water. She grabbed a towel and walked into the house.

"I'm sorry, babe. There's nothing wrong with how you are with Kaila," I said as I followed behind her.

61

"It doesn't seem that way. You and everyone else seems to be bothered by it," Taylor pouted.

"You're thinking way too much into this. Take away what you agree with and try to change and put the rest in the 'Fuck It' box and toss that shit in the cove." She smiled and kissed me.

"Thanks babe, that's good advice."

"I'm good for more than this big D," I said as I wiggled closer to her. I wrapped my arms around her and licked her shoulder.

"You're so nasty," she said as she turned around into a kiss. "I love it." She planted another wet one on me and pulled me toward our bedroom. I hesitated.

"So I'm out of the doghouse?" I asked. Taylor nodded and grinned that let's-get-it-on-grin.

"For now," she added.

"I better bask in this moment. Just in case this bliss doesn't last long," I said with a smile as Taylor guided me to the bedroom where candles were lit and soft music played. "You little sneak, you," I joked as Taylor kissed and undressed me. She pushed me onto the bed and caressed my body with her soft lips. My mind wasn't in the moment. I tried to keep my body into what Taylor wanted and handled. I did my best to please her physically and succeeded.

After a week of anticipation, test day crept up on me sooner than I was prepared for. It fell on a rare day when Taylor and I had a joint day off. Since she had already made plans for us to have a mid-week staycation, there was no way Taylor would accept me cancelling them. Even if she thinks I'm getting called in, she will flip out. I began to casually get dressed, anyway.

"Where do you think you're going?" Taylor asked, swiftly.

"I have to make an appearance at the annual tour our firehouse hosts for the kids. Remember?" Taylor frowned as she tried to remember. Her busy work schedule has made it easier to tell her little white lies --and she believe them. "Kaila was supposed to go but she had a playdate you insisted she couldn't miss."

"Yeah but I also specifically remember that you didn't have to be there," Taylor noted as she grabbed my shirt from off the bed. I stood bare chested as Taylor wound up my blue shirt and slapped me with it. I pretended to flinch and she did it again. I hopped back and snatched the shirt from her.

"You gotta stay ready baby," I teased as I waved the shirt in her face.

"Seriously, though Chris, we have plans. I could've went to work too, you know," Taylor said.

"This won't take long at all. I'll be in and out in no time," I said to reassure her since she didn't look happy.

"Do I have enough time to go to the nail salon? Or enough time to get a quick wash and set...or do I have enough time to do both?"

"Let's just say enough time for both to be on the safe side," I replied.

"I just have to make an appearance at the firehouse," Taylor mocked. "It sounds more like a shift but whatever. If that's how you'd rather spend your day off..." Taylor shrugged then rolled her eyes. I pulled her into a hug. She resisted. I kissed her shoulder. "Just be ready by 2," she said. "Or you're back in the doghouse."

"I'll see you later," I said before I headed out the garage door. I sent a text and pulled off. Fifteen minutes later, I pulled into the fire station's garage. Austynn and Kristian showed up a few minutes after I arrived.

"I'm glad you guys could make it," I said as I opened the car door for Austynn. I opened the back door and extended my hand out to Kristian for a handshake.

"I'm happy to be here, Mr. Chris. Thank you for inviting us," Kristian said, rather maturely for a seven year old. "This is beyond exciting." I smiled at his advanced vocabulary. From the looks of things, Austynn is doing a good job raising him.

"He couldn't stop talking about it," Austynn conversed as we walked into the empty firehouse together.

"Am I the only one?" Kristian asked as he looked around. I glanced at Austynn who smiled and patted Kristian's back.

"Yes! Since your mom knows me, you get a special, private tour. Pretty cool, huh?" The annual tour was actually taking place at another location so I used this location to have some privacy when it was time to take the DNA swab.

"So cool," Kristian responded. He was amazed when I showed Kristian the infamous pole. He had to test it out himself. He slid into the fire truck garage, where there were a fleet of trucks that made Kristian awestruck.

Austynn snapped shots of his priceless expression as he jumped around and hoped from truck to truck. I pointed out the claxon and asked if he wanted to ring it. He nodded with glee. I showed Kristian the rescue dorm where I stay when I work. We went into one of the trucks and treated him as a rescue followed by a demonstration of CPR.

"Would you like to be my volunteer?" I asked Kristian. He nodded his agreeance. He hopped on the gurney and I took his blood pressure. He smiled the entire time. I showed him how to find his own pulse. When Kristian felt like he mastered it, he tried to find Austynn's pulse. I put the oxygen mask over his face and pretended to turn on the tank.

"Ok, one final task. Sometimes patients have to get swabbed. Can I swab the side of your cheek?" Kristian shrugged. He became sullen.

"I did this before," Kristian recalled. Austynn comforted him with a hug.

"Do you want us to get swabbed, too?" She asked. He nodded. As a way to make Kristian feel comfortable, Austynn swabbed the inside of my cheek. I grabbed a q-tip and smiled as I held Austynn's chin in my hand and swabbed alongside the wall of her mouth. I put the DNA samples into test tubes. I fastened the tubes and put them into an envelope.

"You did great," Austynn praised Kristian as he jumped off the gurney. We both filled out the form to include our separate addresses. This way

Austynn and I would receive a copy of the results mailed to us. I put the address form in the same envelope and sealed it. We led Kristian outside as the tour came to an end. Austynn fastened Kristian in the backseat of her car. She kept the door a jar as we waited for the mail carrier to pick up the package.

When the mail carrier arrived she took the package and placed it in a pile on her mail truck. Austynn quickly readied to leave. She looked at her wristwatch and shuffled to the driver's seat of her car.

"I need to get home. I have chicken in the slow cooker," Austynn explained.

"Ok, it was nice to see you," I said once I realized Kristian fell asleep. "We must have tired him out."

"Yeah, we did a lot today," Austynn said as she got ready to pull off. I reached inside my pocket and pulled out my wallet. I handed her a fifty dollar bill. She looked up and smiled.

"You don't have to give me money every time you see us."

"Just accept it and put some gas in your car, buy some snacks for the house and have a little lunch money for him," I said.

"Thank you, Chris," Austynn said as she drove off. I went back inside the firehouse and fell asleep in my dorm. I woke up to six missed calls and two long and angry text messages from Taylor. One questioning where I was and why was it taking so long for me to answer her. The second one cancelled our impromptu staycation. "I decided to reschedule my day off and build my work ethic around the stellar example you have shown me. It's a work thing. I'm sure you understand. I don't know when I'll be home. So don't wait up."

I wondered aloud what could've been important enough for Taylor to reschedule the one thing she claimed was more important than anything - spending time with her man. I got a text from Austynn as soon as I got home thanking me for the day. "Kristian talked about it nonstop since we left. It was so cool."

"It was fun for me, too," I replied.

"When the results come in and you know he's yours, we can do family dates."

"I think it's called family day - and let's cross that bridge when we get there."

"Fair enough. Good night," the message said.

"Likewise," I replied. I walked into an empty house. I called Taylor and to my surprise she picked up. I heard a man's voice in the background. He seemed close enough to Taylor where he and and I could hold a conversation with ease.

"Who's that?" I questioned immediately. I yelled loud enough for her companion to hear.

"That's Jerome," Taylor answered, rather quickly. "He's an accountant at work. You do remember the many times I mentioned his name being that he was one of my first hires," Taylor rationalized.

"I remember," I lied. "When will you be home? It's already 6 p.m. You should've been home by now. I'm ready to eat."

"You're more than welcome to cook yourself something. I won't be home for another hour or so. This dinner meeting isn't over."

"Is your father attending this meeting as well?"

"No." Taylor answered sternly. "He isn't."

"Ok. I guess I'll see you later then," I replied. I hung up with Taylor and called Kaila to say good night. When Kaila was with her grandparents, she went to bed by seven o'clock - eight the latest. After a few minutes of going over my day with Kaila and hearing about hers, I blew kisses and wished my baby a good night.

After a hot shower, I sat on the couch and ate leftover sushi with a cold beer. I searched for a show that would put me to sleep. I woke up to Taylor stumbling up the stairs. I glanced at the hall's wall clock. Midnight. Taylor smiled a sly smile.

"The time just got away from us," she said as she slid out of her heels. Taylor clumsily pulled her pantyhose off of each leg. After her slight struggle to get out of her Ralph Lauren blazer, she threw her blouse into the hamper and shimmied out of her pencil skirt. She made her way to the bathroom for a quick shower then plopped onto bed afterwards, still dripping wet. Taylor released a heavy sigh before getting up to dry herself off and put on her pajamas.

"I hope you know what you're doing," I warned when she got under the duvet.

"I'm just giving you the relationship you've been giving me," she replied as set her alarm to 6:30 a.m. Taylor turned the light switch off on the lamp on the nightstand, then turned her back toward me. "Good night, Chris."

Ray
Fall for Your Type

"Trying to convince myself I've found the one, making the mistake I never learned from."   - Jamie Foxx

Ashley walked into the house with Isaiah and some shopping bags in tow. I was into the kitchen when Isaiah zoomed past me without speaking. I stood in front of the stove cooking up a quick dinner. Ashley kissed me and walked into her bedroom to change into comfortable clothes. "Days off are the best for retail therapy," Ashley said when she re-emerged. "Too bad I got called to go in tonight."

"Open a window," I said as I pulled a golden fillet from the sizzling grease. "Air out that fish smell." Isaiah returned to the kitchen in a Ninja Turtle t-shirt, Batman pajama pants and yellow and orange striped socks.

"Hi Ray," Isaiah said as he sat down at the table to eat.

"Hi little man," I replied. "Are you ready for dinner?" I asked Isaiah as I turned off the burner of the stovetop. I displayed my finished products in the middle of the dining room table as if we were attending a gourmet, catered event.

"I am. What are you making?" Isaiah asked.

"A little bit of fried whiting fillets, some hearty broccoli and one of my favorites - brown rice topped with sauteed peppers and onions," I said with an extravagant gesture and a fancy accent.

"That sounds good," Isaiah said as I shuffled back into the kitchen and grabbed dinnerware. Ashley set the table and began to dish out our food on each plate as I poured her a glass of wine. I sat down at the table with Isaiah.

"Thank you for cooking," Ashley said to me as she sipped the chilled Moscato from her flute.

"Thank you for being born," I responded, adding a kiss. Ashley blushed. "How was your day, baby?" I asked.

"It was good. I think I found my dress. I was just browsing this morning and it kind of stood out. I made an appointment at the boutique in the mall. I think I'm going to order the bridesmaid dresses from there too. It had such a nice selection."

"That's what's up," I said. "Good thing I'm renting my wedding 'fit. Who buys something that they won't ever wear again? Not me. It costs too much. And that doesn't make sense. You may need to Tiffany Haddish the hell out of your dress, as much as you're paying for it."

"How was work for you today," Ashley inquired. I looked up from my plate stuffing my face with a mouthful of food before I answered.

"It was cool," I mumbled. "It was an early day. I just had a few meetings. I went by the house to check on Richie and Shelley."

"Oh, how are they doing?" Ashley asked.

"They weren't there. Shirley said something about class registration. You know they're starting school in August."

"Wow, that's quick. Those two months will be here before you know it."

"Did I tell you that Shirley plans to stay until then?"

"Does that means she will be at the wedding? I already planned for her to be there but you've been insisting that she wouldn't be around," Ashley responded.

"She's doing the best she can right now to stay clean. If being around her children makes that easier this time around, then I welcome it. I'm skeptical but I'm willing to see if Shirley can stay clean."

"Where does she plan on staying?"

"I told her she could stay at the house since I spend most of my time here."

"Do you think that's a good idea?"

"I'm not sure yet. Shirley has been clean for a little while now so we'll see how it goes until she gives me a reason to not believe her anymore. I'll be surprised is she can stay in one spot for six months straight.

"She's known to get bored and we all know what activity Shirley takes up when she's bored." I said as I lifted my pinky finger to my nostril and inhaled.

"Ray, really?" Ashley asked glaring at me. She glanced at Isaiah then back at me. I laughed and shrugged it off.

" Enough about Shirley. Isaiah, how was your day?" I asked him as he pulled apart his fish with a fork.

"Good. I had fun with Mommy at the park. We had ice cream at the mall," he answered as he picked at his dinner plate.

"Are you almost done Isaiah?" Ashley asked him.

"Yes. I'm done now. I don't like fish, I realized," Isaiah expressed as he got up from the table. I got up to help Isaiah empty the scraps leftover on his plate into the garbage disposal. Isaiah put his plate in the dishwasher after I rinsed it off at the sink.

"You realized, huh?" Ashley repeated with a chuckle as she escorted Isaiah into his room. She came out minutes later with a joyful smile. "That child is pure comedy," she said when she sat back at the table. Ashley nibbled a piece of broccoli.

"Are you sure you will be ok staying with him tonight? He should already be asleep by the time I leave. I'm going in around 11 p.m. I could always drop him off with my mom," Ashley declared.

"It's fine. Let him sleep. I can practice daddyhood," I beamed.

"Thank you," she said.

"Anything for you, lady," I replied before we snuggled in the family room. Isaiah ran out of his room waving a DVD cover.

"*Fantasia,*" I said when I finally got a look at the cover art.

"You pulled out a throwback," Ashley said.

"Can we watch this one until I fall asleep," Isaiah whined as he waved the DVD back and forth. Ashley agreed and handed the DVD to me as I put it in the slot on the side of the TV. Isaiah dragged his Spiderman armchair and Snuggie from his room to the family room. Ashley and I cuddled under a throw blanket on the couch.

An hour later, Isaiah's head hung along the back of his chair. I carried him to his room to tuck him in. When I returned to the living room, Ashley had her eyes closed and her mouth open. She exhaled a small snore. I grabbed a pillow and spooned behind her.

I took out my cell phone to scroll through Onblast.com. I sifted through the private messages in my inbox. Most of them were unread messages from Alana, asking questions like, "Where you been?" and attempting to get a response by sliding in a smooth, "I hope you're doing well," statement.

The most recent was from a week ago. "I know you're in a serious relationship now or whatever but you could answer back. We ain't over that easy," the message said. I left those messages unread like I did the rest. Alana will, eventually, get the hint.

A few hours later, Ashley's alarm blasted Blaze 101.1 FM late night radio show. She groggily stretched as she got off the couch. Ashley walked into the bedroom to change into her work clothes. I was amazed at the stamina she had to work the night shift.

"Tell me how ready you are for the fitting tomorrow?" Ashley asked me as she stepped one foot into her scrub pants. After stepping into the other side, she wiggled her big booty into her pants as she pulled up her uniform.

"As ready as I could be. Who else is supposed to be there? You know, besides my crew," I said as I watched her get dressed for another night shift in the emergency room.

"Who is your crew?" Ashley asked as she applied brown liner to her lips. "Are you nervous?" She finished her light makeup look with a swatch of shimmery glitter gloss.

"Mikey and Richie will be there. That's all I need. And why would I be nervous? I'm the coolest under pressure. That's when I thrive."

"Isaiah and Papa Harold, Mr. Jax and Chris," Ashley answered.

"The infamous," I opined. "Why is Chris everywhere? Chris is always around. Why is he going to be there?"

"He's in the wedding. He's my best man," Ashley said and laughed out loud. "Oh yeah, don't forget I'm going to need your half deposit for the venue. They held the date with my half and your $500 will confirm the booking. It's a deal to book the Providence Ballroom at the Omni for that price at such short notice."

"I'll make sure you have that measly $500 - and then some," I reassured her with a kiss. As soon as I heard the alarm secured as Ashley left for work, I reached for my cell phone and texted Mikey to confirm his attendance at the fitting tomorrow. with the proof I needed to reassure Ashley she was marrying the right guy, even though I wasn't all the way sure.

Mikey stood against the brick building waiting for me. We walked toward the car. He put his hand on my shoulder and chuckled. I looked at him out the corner of my eye hoping he wouldn't make a big deal about what we were doing.

"I'm surprised she still doesn't know," Mikey said as he handed me two envelopes with four backdated pay stubs. "I guess what she doesn't know..."

"Won't hurt her," I said as I skimmed through the papers.

"She'll kill you, though," Mikey said. "I know Kennedy would kill me if she knew about my involvement in this." I chuckled at the thought of my past time with Kennedy. And her time with Kelvin before that. Mikey still doesn't know he's married to a pass-around chick.

"How's Kennedy doing, anyway?" I asked politely to change the subject.

"She's fine. She's due soon." Mikey beamed with excitement and pride. "And you would never guess who we saw at her appointment." Mikey paused before blurting out, "Alana! And King...she looked pregnant."

"Oh really," I said. "Well, good for her. She finally found someone to be with."

"She kept asking about you though," Mikey noted.

"Oh yeah?" I smirked. "Alana is...a lost girl. How is she pregnant by another man yet still asking about me?"

"She said she was due in September. Wouldn't that make her six months pregnant?" Mikey got excited about this as if he was watching a novela plot unravel in front of his eyes. I shrugged.

"I'm not keeping track of her. I couldn't tell you."

"Well, maybe you should. Six months ago you were dealing with her," Mikey asserted.

"Six months ago I stopped dealing with her," I corrected. "That baby could be anybody's baby."

"Well, maybe you should give her a call. You might have some unfinished business you need to take care of before you get married. Speaking of which, how are you going to pay for all of this wedding with no job?"

"I will figure something out. You know with these dimples I can get away with just about anything. Hell, Ashley might just pay for the whole wedding by her damn self," I said with a chuckle.

"The real Ray finally resurfaces! Where you been?" Mikey asked.

"I'm always me. And I just had a revelation," I said.

"Oh yeah? What is that?

"This is the end," I said.

"The end of?" Mikey asked still confused.

"The charade. If Ashley wants to be with me like she claims then she'll be ok with me not having a job."

"I don't think any woman is ok with their man being jobless for such an avoidable reason. You didn't have to go to Vegas as her plus one - knowing the rules. You brought that firing on yourself, my brother."

"Ashley will probably just postpone the wedding..." I said, almost sure of her love for me.

"Or dump you altogether. Have you thought about that?"

"Never," I replied with confidence.

"Raymond King, you never cease to amaze me," Mikey stated.

"Maybe that's what you're hoping for," I said. "You don't want to believe I'm in this for the better."

"I know you, man. And any real woman's reaction would be to dump you! I really thought you loved this one," Mikey said sarcastically as though he knew my motives behind my latest revelation.

"I love me more than anyone, Mikey," I reassured. "My mama taught me that."

We walked into the fancy wedding shop. The host guided us to the area where our party gathered. Ashley's stepfather, Harold and Isaiah were already dressed in their suits. Isaiah ran to me and wrapped his arms around my leg as Harold tried on a white tuxedo jacket with black lapels and a polka dot bow tie. He walked over to us and shook my hand.

"You guys are looking sharp already!" I said. Isaiah posed in a velvet suit jacket and a black bow tie. "Let me see what's in here for the man of honor. You know I'm known for my expensive taste."

I retreated to review the rest of the suit jacket selection for Mikey and Richie, who sat in big brown leather arm chairs, in the waiting area, awkwardly jamming to the classical music that played. Mr. Jaxon began to walk toward me. He stood in front of me as I picked out a pair of all black one-button velvet jackets for my guys to try on. I opted to wear a Sean John classic-fit velvet sport coat in dark red with a black bow tie and black slacks.

"You do remember our deal," Mr. Jax whispered in a stern tone. I smiled and nodded. I grabbed two wine red velvet tuxedo jackets for Mikey and Richie to model.

"I thought I had six more months of living rent free," I said as I motioned Mikey and Richie over to me. I attempted to walk away when Mr. Jack grabbed my arm and pulled me back.

"Well...being that you don't have a job," he said. I wrestled my bicep out of his grip. I handed Mikey and Richie the jackets and told them to try them on. "I just want to make sure we're on the same page."

"Come out and show everyone," I said to them. I smiled to release any weird vibes they could sense as Mikey and Richie walked away. I turned back toward Mr. Jax. I looked him directly in his eyes.

"I'm working on getting my job back. In the meantime, I'd appreciate if you keep this between us. Ashley and I are getting married in December. That's when our one-year rent-free deal is up. I will have another job by then," I reassured him. "I swear." We remained locked into this stare down with Mr. Jax until Harold tapped my shoulder and motioned for me to follow him.

"Let's have a conversation," Harold said as he walked ahead of me. Harold was a brown-skinned man in his mid-fifties but could easily pass for mid-forties. He hadn't aged like the rest of his generation, zombie-like similar to how Shirley looks now. He had a salt and pepper beard and all of his hair; hairline still intact. Harold sported a Caesar haircut with deep waves and was fit for an older guy. He had a protruding beer belly that slightly poked out forcing him to use suspenders to keep his pants up. Harold turned to me and placed the palm of his hand on my shoulder.

"I know your type Ray. I used to be you," he said as he began to squeeze. "I swear to you, if you hurt Ashley," he said, tightening his grip. "You'll have to answer to me. Ashley is special. And I expect you to treat her as such."

"I know she's special. That's why I'm marrying her," I replied trying to pretend his gesture didn't hurt. I took a deep breath and glanced at the other guests, who were busy sipping champagne and flirting with the sales reps.

"That better be the reason," Harold said as he squeezed tighter. "Because if you're not prepared to take care of her, I'll make sure she's not taking care of you. Do you understand what I'm saying?" Harold asked. I laughed as he released his grip. I began to rub my shoulder and neck.

"Marriage is 50/50," I protested.

"No it's not." Harold emphathesized with my ignorance by shaking his head. "It's about being there for her through her toughest moments, loving her beyond her hair not being done and her un-pedicured feet. Loving her past the physical. Love her, full of the flaws and imperfections God gave her. Are you ready for that type of commitment?"

"I think so," I said, hesitantly.

"You need to be sure. Marriage is about loving the commitment more than the person you're committed to. That love will enhance her to become a better partner to do life with. So any man who claims to love Ashley must accept that she is a queen and the man marrying her has to treat her that way. Anything less will diminish her true potential. And would you really wouldn't want to answer to all of the men in her life should you choose to disappoint."

"We all know my name is King. I'm royalty in real life. And Ashley is *my* queen. It's only fitting I treat her as such. You have my word."

"I hope your word means something to you," Harold said. "Because your words mean nothing to me if your actions do not match. Remember that."

We finished trying clothes on as we joked and laughed. I downed the remainder of the champagne as Harold and Jax split the bill. I accepted their gesture with open arms, considering I wasn't prepare to spend any money.

"Don't disappoint me," Harold said as we left the building.

"I'll do my best," I reassured him.

"Do better than your best," he whispered as he shook my hand.

Later that night, I returned to Ashley's house. With Isaiah off to bed, Ashley and I cuddled up in the living room watching reruns of *The Fresh Prince of Bel-Air*. I looked at Ashley as she giggled at a Carlton joke.

"Your laugh is sexy as hell," I complimented. "When are you going to give me some," I wondered out loud.

"Um...did we get married yet?" Ashley shot back. I just looked at her out the corner of my eye. She smiled. "Exactly. So since that answer is no...my answer is still no. And you know exactly why you haven't gotten any yet," I reminded him.

"Yeah because you're a prude," I noted. "You know you're messing up my image, right? I'm a King out here in these streets. You're tainting my good name," I joked.

"Messing up your image? Tainting your good name?" Ashley repeated, flabbergasted. "Being known as a player is not something to be proud of," Ashley insisted. "You're damn near 30. It's time to grow up, don't you think? Besides that you told me that me being celibate was fine with and you had no problem waiting. You did propose, you know, already knowing I am celibate. And you made our engagement public by doing it during the bank auction and then with the whole Onblast.com announcement. So know you want to go back to being a player?"

"I'm not a player...you know the rest," I proclaimed.

"So you're cheating on me?" she asked.

"No. Not at the moment," I replied. "But after the lectures I got from Mr. Jack and Harold today, I'm starting to wonder where the benefits are. You're really making it hard for me."

"I know," she said. "But you love me so you'll wait." Ashley leaned in closer and kissed my neck. She looked at me with her big, beautiful hazel eyes and smiled until that deep dimple showed. And for some reason, she was right.

"Wait, what did Harold have on? I told him he had to stay away from suspenders. He always has on suspenders. I want him to look elegant and less like his daily business wear."

"He had on suspenders," I broke it to her. She laughed. I smiled. This level of intimacy was intense. I was drawn to her. It was magnetic. I leaned in for a kiss and she met me halfway. My green eyes mirrored her hazels. I grabbed her cheeks into the palm of my hands and pulled her into a passionate kiss.

"I love you so much, Ashley," I said. "You're such a good person. You keep it real. You're mysterious. And sexy as hell. The crazy thing is you're more beautiful inside than you are on the outside and that's pretty asf." Ashley blushed as I continued to compliment.

"You're the best thing that ever happened to me. If we never have sex - know and understand that!"

"Ok, Ray. You say that now and I really hope that's how you feel when life happens. You know, when the not-so-good parts show up and stay longer than anyone is comfortable with."

"I'm with you forever, baby. No amounts of ups or downs can change that," I said after I kissed her again. "For better or worse remember. So I'll wait for sex...for now," I said as my phone vibrated in my pocket. I pulled it out to view the screen and slid it back inside my pocket.

"Who are you ignoring?" Ashley asked.

"Nobody important," I replied. "Everyone gets put on hold when I'm with my baby." I kissed Ashley again, who pulled back. "And I got something to tell you while I have the courage," I said. I could tell she grew suspicious. I had to figure out a way to tell her about not having a job before she finds out on her own. She leaned against the armrest of the couch and pulled a pillow to her chest.

"You got a secret girlfriend I should know about?" Ashley asked half joking.

"What? No. That's a secret I wouldn't be able to keep. Girls love me too much to stay quiet about me wifing them up."

"What about a secret baby?" Ashley asked nonchalantly.

"What kind of question is that? I am marrying the mother of my child, first off, just like my daddy did, so don't even play like that," I snapped. "Lucky for you that's not an issue because I'm conceited with mine. I won't just raw it with anyone. And besides, you are the one only woman I see myself having kids with. I just want you to know that I got

79

you...no matter what," I said before I pulled out five Benjamins. "I've been working to make sure we're straight for now and our future," I mislead as I handed Ashley two backdated pay stubs. "I'm serious about one person...and that's you. I really love you."

"I'm glad to hear that," she said as she happily accepted the cash. "But you're still not getting any for another six months. So just hold tight. December will be here before you know it."

"Geesh. Eight months. Well, you can't blame a brother for trying," I said adding a kiss.

Ashley
Take Care
"You hate the fact that you bought the dream when they sold you one..." - Drake

Cake tasting and menu sampling day was finally on the agenda for the night and I was beyond excited. Ray, on the other hand, was unenthusiastic. As I ranted and raved about the catering options, Ray was quiet and repressed. I could sense tension emitting off of him when I picked him up. He didn't engage in any of the small talk I initiated. He turned the volume of the radio louder to avoid any further conversation.

Once we arrived, Ray disputed the price of everything I set my eyes on. Before he tasted anything, he said, "that looks expensive," with disdain. Out of all the flavors I picked, Ray asked the baker to taste "the cheapest version" of those same flavors only to dislike them all. I tried to hide my embarrassment when Ray offered his sister's baking skills up for our big day.

While I was offended, the baker didn't seem moved or upset, nor did the wedding coordinator as they both expressed dealing with these types of debates during other couples' tastings.
We returned home from the cake tasting a little after nine. Ray retreated into the bedroom as if he'd been out past his curfew.

"I loved the red velvet. The cream cheese frosting was delicious. I can still taste it. And she said she could get the red to match perfectly with the bridesmaids' dresses," I said when I bombarded into the bedroom. When Ray didn't respond, I continued planning our wedding aloud. I knew he was concerned about money, but with both of us working, the budget should not inflate to a point where we can't afford it. I tried to reassure him of that - to no avail.

"You do know my parents offered to pay for the wedding cake and there's a $1,000 budget for that. And Mr. Jack and Ms. Amy agreed to pay for the remaining balance of the catering balance" I reminded him. Somehow, that still didn't satisfy Ray when it came to us splurging for our special day. He still hadn't really given me much to go off of since we returned. But I continued to talk him out of his funk.

"Let's go over what's left to do," I enthused. "The dresses are ordered. The catering menu has been confirmed. The florist said the flowers will have to be flown in because they are out of season."

"Are you still thinking of a live band that plays hip hop? Or can we go with a DJ? I can get Manny to do it for free. It's the least he can do," Ray said, finally nonce.

"You say that like he owes you something," I noted. "What do you think about a limo? Or a horse and carriage, pulling up like Cinderella." I got excited at the thought.

"How much is that going to cost us? It's going to be December. Do you really want to torture that poor animal with pulling us through snow and cold weather?"

"If they can ride horse through the snowy mountains in Game of Thrones then…" I shrugged. "I think these New England horses will manage winter weather."

"You do know that show is make believe, not real, all fake?" Ray pointed out as he shook his head. "Did you confirm the appointment with the jeweler? I'm ready to bling you out. Where's Isaiah tonight?"

"He's at the Blackstone tonight with his grands. I swear he loves being over there more than he likes being home with his own mother. The life of having wealthy grandparents," I said with a sigh. "Lucky kid."

"So Isaiah's with Mr. Jaxon tonight. That's great," Ray said. I could hear a hint of irritation as he spoke. "He is over there a lot. You should keep him home more," Ray expressed.

"I think it's good for him to be in the presence of his father's family even if Eric isn't around," I reasoned.

"If you say so," Ray said. "I thought we were going to talk about what's left to do. We haven't talked about our vows."

I sat back and smiled as Ray showcased a real interest in expressing his feelings for me. It was so gratifying to have Ray love on me without it getting physical first - it was almost was an aphrodisiac. I knew now would be the best time to open up since I could sense the seriousness of his feelings for me and they were genuine.

"Do you want to do something traditional?" I proposed, basking in the conversation. "Or do you want to write your own."

"I want to start with the traditional vows like honor and, especially obey, sickness and health, till death parts us but I want to do my own thing too, like 'Seeing that booty switch through the lobby of my job's building had me stuck from the start.' You know? Like, 'Ashley is the best thing that has ever happened to me and I only want to spend the rest of my life honoring that fact.' I'm trying to have all of the women in tears and all of the men...a standing ovation."

"You gotta stop doing that?" I said as I hung onto every word he said. With Ray, my feelings were different.

We had a magnetizing connection but I proceeded with caution. But I found myself pleasantly surprised. Ray's rough exterior is just an armour to shield his softer heart.

"What?" He noticed my gaze.

"Saying things that make me want to kiss you," I stated as I leaned in to plant a seductive one on Ray, which surprised him - only for a second. He immediately switched to ready. We began kissing and breathing heavily, letting the mood dominate our bodies. His fingertips branded my thigh as he pulled me closer to him. Every soft-lipped kiss made my willpower melt like butter in a hot skillet. The chemistry between us was hair-standing electric. His mere presence was euphoric and any slight touch gave me goosebumps.

"Please," he whispered into my ear before he bit my earlobe, skyrocketing the sexual tension that filled the room. I pulled back from his grasp and grabbed his chin into the palm of my hands. I gazed into his green eyes and bit my bottom lip. He pulled my shirt off and latched onto my nipple that peeked out the top of my bra cup. I squirmed and moaned, with resistance. When Ray's hand ventured into my panties and I suddenly remembered that I had my celibacy rule.

"I want you," I said as I jumped up. "But we can't. I can't. I'm sorry. I got too excited about this wedding. I guess the planning is turning me on but I'm just...I'm just not ready to go there yet." Ray sighed heavily. He leaned against the headboard.

"Your body is ready," Ray said as he rubbed his fingers together. "Come on. Just let your freak flag fly, baby," Ray preached.

He kissed my neck. I almost gave in. I pulled away and sat on the edge of the bed. "What's stopping you?"

"You."

"Please elaborate," he insisted with raised his eyebrows. I offended him.

"I'm just cautious. You know how dudes are. I don't know if you're really serious about me and the fact that we don't really know each other. I am being the responsible one. I'm not sure what you're really doing when you're not around me," I pointed out. "How do I know if you're not out sleeping with everybody?"

"Because I'm here with you every night, damn near begging you to give Prince some attention. You walk around with lace panties and a tank top hanging off your shoulder. I could see your nipples poking through your shirt. You never wear a bra! Knowing how much I am attracted to you and I'm supposed to just...ugh, wait! I don't know. It's crazy. It's like whenever we get close to making progress you pull back. I'm just not used to girls doing that...and when they do it's usually a reason for it. Like another man, a yeast infection or something that don't got nothing to do with whatever their excuse was."

"If you really want to know...there is a reason but I'm not sure if you're ready to hear it."

"What is it?"

"I've had a lot of things happen as a result of having sex...so I'm skeptical of opening up to anyone because of it. I know some things scare people out the door and I'm not ready to lose you," I confessed.

"First of all, where am I going if I want to marry you? And secondly, what could you possibly tell me that will make me leave you?" Ray grabbed my hand. "You can tell me anything," he said. I cleared my throat to stop my voice from shaking as I prepared to tell my future husband my most shameful flaw.

"I have herpes," I whispered.

"Excuse me?" Ray said with confusion. "I thought I heard you and herpes." Ray tried to make eye contact. I looked away. I swallowed hard and cleared my throat again.

"You heard me correctly. I do have herpes," I bashfully admitted.

"Excuse me?" Ray repeated. He sat with his hand over his mouth. After a few minutes of silence, the initial shock wore off. "Damn. That's crazy. I would've never thought," Ray finally said once he recovered from the news. "It's always the ones you would never expect. Is that why you're celibate? Damn. So how long did you have it? When did you find out you had it? Do you know who gave it to you?"

"I do. I dated this guy, Jay-J, a few years ago. It's almost been four years ago. Isaiah was turning two when we met. He'll be six soon. Anyway, we dated for almost a year. When I thought things were starting to get serious between us, Jay-J told me he was moving to Alabama. He started being distant and acting funny and one day he slipped up. He called me from his house - and when I returned the call, his fiancée answered the phone."

Ray was stunned. He hung onto my every word. He listened closer than he would if I was an announcer at a Celtics game. The story of my vaginal demise was mega entertaining to him. He ooed and awed with every revealed secret. "I met his secret fiancé who revealed that Jay-J was engaged to be married, had a baby that he pretended to be his niece and was the one who actually had herpes and pretended that I was the one who gave it to him. Ugh. It was crazy and I'm glad it's over."

"Wow. I'm so sorry to hear that someone would do you like that. That man took your choice away. He made you deal with him based off a lie and tried to leave you like a coward.

"How do could he take away someone else's choice? I mean, I've done a lot of fucked up things, but nothing like that. That's beyond petty. I'm mad at him for you. How could he do that to my future wife? I wish I could've saved you from that hurt." Ray rubbed my arm and held my hand. I was touched to tears when I heard Ray's comforting words.

Ray still feels like I'm his future wife even though I just spilled my most shameful secret. "It's like I'm so sad for you and so happy you didn't do me the same way. Like you could be vengeful and take it out on everybody...but you told me." I just nodded. "You could've turned into a hoe but you took the high road."

"Jay-J definitely stole my choice. He could've told me but I understand why he didn't," I replied.

"He knew I would not have had sex with him so carefreely if he had told me about his infectious penis and that's exactly what he didn't want. But I did like him. How he chose to deal with his demons was out of my control."

"Agreed but you didn't have to be collateral damage, either. He could've used a condom."

"Trust me, I know. I've thought of all the scenarios. I could've insisted more that he did use a condom, too. I just would've rather been able to make my own decision instead of getting lied to for months only to find out he never had any real intention of having anything real with me."

"I just want you to know I understand that this was difficult for you, but I appreciate you telling me. I don't look at you any different. I actually am impressed with your courage and strength. I swear you amaze me, everyday."

"Well that's good to hear," I said, relieved. "I have been afraid to tell you but I think everyone deserves honesty. I'm sorry it took me so long to let you in."

"What happened to him? Have you seen him since?" Ray pulled me closer to him. He wrapped his arms around me.

"I spotted him a few times. But I haven't communicated with him. And I still haven't gotten a genuine apology. I don't really need closure. Whatever happened...happened. The real issue I had with Jay-J was how much time he put into pretending to be someone he wasn't. He gave me a whole story about moving away to cover up that he was getting married. It was lie after lie after lie and everything finally came out."

"Wow. I'm sorry you had to go through with that," Ray sympathized. "And I applaud you for being open with me. It just makes me have more respect for you. Because you didn't steal me," Ray said just as relieved as I was that he wasn't freaking out. He pulled a tissue from the box and wiped my tears away.

"I still feel some kind of way too about not getting any," he said trying to make me laugh. "But I think I have a better understanding of your hesitation when it comes to us taking our relationship sexual."

"Our wedding day will be here before you know it," I said as I sniffled. "And this whole celibacy rule will be a thing of the past."

"Ugh," he said with a pout. "I still think December is too long," Ray said as he began to rub my lower back. He kissed the arch.

"Don't get any ideas. I still have my celibacy rule," I reminded him.

"Rules are meant to be broken, you know," Ray said with a sly smile. He leaned back. "I know if I kiss you, I wouldn't be able to stop," he revealed. We both laughed. "The problem is I'm starting to get sexually frustrated."

"Trust me, I can relate. Just because I'm adamant about this no-sex until marriage thing, doesn't mean I don't crave sex. I just am able to fight my temptation. I want a happy, sex-filled marriage more than I want to scratch a temporary itch."

"Sex-filled marriage? How much are we talking about here? Five days a week?"

"Every time you want it...however you want it, wherever you want it," I said.

"You better not be lying," Ray said with a laugh. Ray kissed my cheek. "I have work in the morning. Let's get some rest."

"Can you rub my back?" I asked. Ray sighed but obliged. "I'm sorry about not telling you sooner. I should've told you a long time ago."

"It's all good, Ashley. I can only imagine how hard it was for you to tell me. I'm glad you did. We're good. Now let's go to sleep," Ray said. He gave me another kiss and rubbed my back until we both fell asleep.

The next morning I woke up to an empty bed. I noticed Ray's clothes were gone. I walked into the kitchen to ready-made breakfast and a note:

I'll see you later, baby. Enjoy them eggs. You owe me!

I giggled and nibbled a piece of the cold eggs on the plate. I put the plate into the microwave for a thirty-second jolt. As I waited, I grabbed my cell and called Taylor. She didn't answer so I dialed Morgan's number.

"Whats up girl?" Morgan spouted in a rushed voice.

"How busy are you?"

"I'm busy. I'm on assignment until next week. Can it wait until then? It's not code red, is it?"

"No. It's more like yellow so I guess it's going to have to wait," I said with sigh.

"Ok, not serious but too pressing," Morgan recited our yellow definition to our gossip code of severity. Back in college, along with Ladies Night, we came up with this gossip code that would rate the severity level of vent mode needed by one of us. Our three level codes were very similar to the government terror alert, using red for an immediate need to stop everything and orange meant one of us was in need of a call of at least fifteen minutes. "I swear I'll call you back. I'm on the way to meet one of my sources."

"It's fine. I understand. It can actually wait until our next Ladies Night. Go chase that story. We'll talk soon," I said.

"You sure, I have a few minutes," Morgan estimated. "Like exactly...three minutes."

"No it's fine," I conceded.

"Did you call Taylor," Morgan asked through her distractions.

"I did. She's too busy to answer now that she's got her new job and all. I just need to get myself busy and start my day," I said. "I still have to pick up Isaiah. And run a few errands anyway so we'll talk soon. You get back to work and I'll track you down later," I concluded as I hung up the phone with Morgan. I finished my breakfast and headed out to pick up Isaiah from his grandparents house.

Their eight bedroom waterfront mansion was the biggest house in the Blackstone neighborhood. It sat on two acres of family-owned land and stood at nearly 10,000 square feet. The curb appeal was spectacular from the circular driveway.

As I rounded the curve of the driveway, I passed my favorite part of their property, the garden. Giant arborvitae evergreens bordered the endless rows of hibiscus, hydrangea blooms, water lilies and a plethora of other exotic plants.
I nearly bumped into the bumper of Miss Amy's new seven series beamer as I pulled behind her to park, leering in awe. I walked to the red door that Mr. Jax turns into Santa every Christmas season and rang the bell. Miss Amy answered to the door, seemingly surprised to see me. She was probably just was surprised as I was to see her answer her own door. Usually, their in-house chef, Michelle, answers.

The Blackstone, as we nicknamed the mansion back in the day, was magnificent, elegant and regal - from the glass chandeliers to the gold-encrusted crown molding, vaulted ceilings and a fireplace in every room. I stood in the foyer as Isaiah ran down the stairs and jumped into my open arms.

"I missed you," I said as I squeezed him tight until he squirmed free. "Are you ready to come home like I'm ready for you to be there?"

"I can't, sorry. We're going to Paris tonight, Mom," Isaiah responded nonchalantly.

"You have a vivid imagination, my love," I said with . "Go get your things baby, we've got things to do today."

"Ashley, you know we love Isaiah," Miss Amy asked. I nodded. "We want him to stay with us since you have more things to do. He can afford to miss daycare. He's smarter than the teacher."

"Stay? For how long?"

"Through the weekend. Just tell them he's on vacation. We are headed out of the country, adding more stamps to our passport pages."

"Where are you and the mister off to now? I swear you have the best life."

"We're going to Paris, tonight."

"And you want Isaiah to go out of the country? Do you really want a 5-year old on vacation with you and your husband? Grandchild or not, that's a little intrusive."

"Kaila will be there, too. I'm surprised Taylor didn't tell you. She usually tells you everything. Have you talked to her?"

"She's been busy with her new job and all. We are overdue for some girl time."

"Taylor doesn't need to work but if she insists," Ms. Amy said with a shrug. "You know? Not everyone can have a lifestyle like this."

"Right," I agreed. "This is definitely something *anyone* can get accustomed to."

"That's why you should let Isaiah come with us," Ms. Amy argued. They traveled a lot and whenever they could they would bring their grands for the 'experience.'

"Where are you guys off to this time?"

'Paris for the week," Miss Amy spat nonchalantly. "If not the remainder of the summer. It would be just fine for him to miss a week or two from childcare. You know Mister Jax's motto: family first." I wasn't persuaded. "What if Isaiah goes with you now and I'll stop by to pick him up later," Ms. Amy suggested. "And this gives you some extra alone time with your new fiancé." Ms. Amy did make a good point.

"There's a thought," I said. "Or I can go to work and take advantage of this overtime so I can pay for this wedding," I noted.

"Well, you don't have to. We can take care of whatever you need. You're like a daughter to us."

"Thank you. I appreciate the offer but the cake was pricey enough and you're already handling that. But I will let you know if I need to use the family name to pull some strings," I said with a laugh.

"Say no more," Ms. Amy said. "Whenever you need us, just give one of us a call. And don't be too proud to ask."

"Hey...once the offer is extended," I said with a shrug. We both chuckled. Ms. Amy walked into the large, restaurant style kitchen. I followed behind her and sat down on a leather bar stool at the island. Ms. Amy fixed herself an Ace of Spades bellini from a glass pitcher and offered me one. I nodded and Ms. Amy poured until my wine flute was full. After my first sip, I spent another few minutes in thought, I came to a decision.

"I wouldn't want Isaiah to miss out on such an opportunity because I want him with me due to my loneliness...so it's fine," I insisted.

"Isaiah can go to Paris. While I get to go pick out some linens and finalize this menu," I said. "He can go with you to Paris. I'll just have to say my goodbyes now."

"And of course, you don't have to worry about anything. We'll take care of Isaiah's clothes and travel expenses. Isaiah," Ms. Amy called out. Isaiah scurried down the stairs with his Black Panther backpack dragging behind him. He had his blanket hanging from out of his bag with other garments stuffed behind it. He walked up to me and pointed to his jacket that fell on the bottom step of the staircase. I pulled Isaiah into a long hug. I smelled his hair and kissed his head.

91

"Have fun on your trip. Pretty soon you'll have more stamps on your passport than me," I said. Isaiah's eyes widened and he pulled away from our hug.

"Can we go see the waffle tire?" Isaiah enthused with excitement. Ms. Amy and I laughed, which confused Isaiah.

"I think you mean Eiffel Tower," I corrected. He did not flinch.

"That's what I said," he maintained. I laughed again. Isaiah dropped his bag at his feet and ran to Michelle, who just finished making him a homemade coconut banana ice cream sundae.

"I'll call you later to say goodnight Isaiah. Enjoy yourself and don't forget to behave," I said after I finally got my goodbye kiss.

As I headed out the door, I said my goodbyes to the rest of the family and prayed for their safe travels. I received a reminder alert from my phone. It was a calendar event for a table linen appointment I booked four weeks ago. I glanced at the clock. I was close to the shop so I texted Ray to remind him to meet me there.

I pulled up at exactly a half an hour before the appointment and waited for Ray to show up. I sent Ray a reminder text. No response. Another set of unanswered texts, three ignored phone calls and fifteen minutes later, I went in without him. I spent thirty minutes discussing the pros and cons of cloth table linens versus disposable plastic ones to a science. Regardless, I based my entire decision on the cheapest price.

Two hundred and fifty dollars later, I pushed through the double wooden doors of the linen shop backwards. As I spun around and bumped right into someone who walked the sidewalk.

"Oh my goodness, I'm such a klutz. I'm sorry. I should've pushed the door open the right way," I said as I turned around. When I lifted my head I noticed the man's face. I tried to casually walk away before he noticed me.

"Well, well well...if it isn't Ashley Jay," the familiar face said as he leaned in for a hug.

"Yup, it's me," I said as I pulled back from his gesture and cut my eyes at him. He quickly got the hint and kept his distance - but blocked my path to my car. I peered over his shoulder toward where I parked and tried to come up with an escape plan. This is one encounter I wasn't ready to have. We both stood there, momentarily in an awkward silence. He smiled again.

"I read about your wedding posted at Onblast.com. Congratulations. When's the big day?"

"Thank you. We're getting married on Christmas Day," I chuckled. "That way I could remember my birthday for more than your wedding day."

"Me and Jess never made that walk down the aisle. We're still together, you know, just trying to figure things out," Jay-J said in a sullen tone.

"You may have to stop cheating on her, keeping her a secret and claim your child with her...that might help you figure things out. I'm just saying," I said with a shrug. I started to walk toward my car. Jay-J turned around to walk beside me.

"I just wanted to tell you that I'm happy that you finally found love...you know considering," Jay-J said.

"Considering, what exactly?"

"You know?"

 "Oh, you thought you would mess up my chances? You thought I would never find someone to look past what you did to me?"

"I didn't mean it like that," he said as voice faded into a whisper.

"Of course, they never do," I retorted. "Listen, thank you for the congratulations but I really have somewhere to be. Excuse me," I said as I sat in the car and slammed the door shut. I let out a deep breath before I fastened my seatbelt and turned the ignition. Jay-J glared at me through the window before he tapped on it to get my attention. I sighed. I silently debated if I wanted to hear anything else he had to say. I rolled down the window.

"You know it's too bad we didn't work out. I know you really cared about me," Jay-J revealed. "You were a good woman, Ashley. It's crazy, you know, the timing of everything. I had a lot going on, when we met."

"Yeah a new baby, a fiance and a disease is a hell of a lot," I said. Jay-J slightly rolled his eyes.

"All I'm saying is...if we would've met at a different time, I think we could've really been good together."

"Yeah," I paused. "I'm not so sure if I agree. Things worked out just how they were supposed to. Because even though I cared about you deeply, I didn't really know you, at all. And everything between us was a lie. Your secret engagement, hidden newborn and a lifelong disease that you infected me with...could've been overlooked. You made me think I was the one who gave you something. You would make it seem like I was the problem, when it was really you. You were a dirty liar who had a whole family that you hid for your own selfish reasons. You are the only thing that killed any chances of us working out." Jay-J didn't say anything. He just stood there, looking somewhat sad, which was unbelievable, considering he lacks affect.

"So, I'm glad we didn't work out, actually," I realized out loud. "Now, if you'll excuse me," I said with a smirk as I pulled off. I left Jay-J standing in the street.

On my way home, I attempted to reach Ray for the tenth time since leaving the Blackstone mansion. He didn't answer. Over the next few days, Ray didn't answer any phone calls or return any text messages. It didn't matter what time of the day I sent them or the content of them - he wasn't responding. I started to worry more about his safety. *Should I pop up at his house?*

I quickly dismissed that idea because if a chick is there...who knows how I would react. The number of possibilities I would be opening myself up to were endless. I sent one last text, expressing myself, no filter.

"You just disappear for days now? You could've told me
you needed space or some time to wrap your head around

94

what I told you. Something would be better than you
disappearing and ignoring me. It's all good though. I
understand. If space is what you need...I'll give you that."

I typed the message but hesitated to send it. When I built up the nerve
I hit the send button before I lost it. I checked the phone constantly
expecting Ray's reply. Still no response.

I turned the phone over and tucked it under my pillow. A little after
midnight a text alert vibrated through the pillow. I grabbed it.

"You think everything is about you, huh?
I have way more to worry about than what
you told me. I'm ok thanks for asking and
yes, I needed space. There's more. I'll
explain everything later. Dinner at your
place? Does six o'clock work for you? I
know you miss me. I'll call you around five
for the reminder. I love you, Ashley."

At nine o'clock the next morning, I received Ray's usual "hello
beautiful" text message. I didn't respond and he called me right away.
I didn't answer the first time to see if he would call back. He did. I
answered on the second ring.

"Well, well, well... if it isn't the infamous missing-in-action fiancé of
mine," I sassed.

"Hello to you, too, beautiful," Ray said as if we were on good terms.
"We can talk more about that later. You don't have to sass me. Just
say you missed me. I'll be home later tonight and by home I mean your
house, after you go pick up the pizza I'm going to order from Fellini's.
And I'll tell you everything so you can't be mad at me anymore."

"I like your nerve," I noted. "How do you just invite yourself over like
that?"

"That was smooth right," Ray said with a laugh. "Seriously, though. I
know it's been a few days since we've been on the same page, but
you need to know what I'm about to tell you...if you want to move
forward. I don't want to keep you too much longer, I know you're
working. I just wanted to hear your voice, beautiful."

95

"You're not that smooth Ray," I assured him. "I'm not sure about tonight. I may have to work overtime. I'll text you around 5:30 to see if you're still this friendly."

"Girl for you, I'll be friends with Jesus," Ray said adding a laugh.

"You may need to call him to save you because you're so far gone," I said with a sly laugh. "I can't with you...do you really think you can invite yourself over to my house after you ignored me for the past week."

"You're exaggerating. It's only been five days," he said.

"It's been four," I corrected.

"See," Ray said. "I know you missed me. Just let me come over and explain. If you don't believe my reasoning then I will leave -- no problem. But we both know that's not what you want."

"Someone is really feeling themself today. You out here stroking your own ego?"

"I can't wait to see your face when I break it to you and then you're going to be so mad at yourself for ever doubting me...it's going to be great. So, are we on for tonight or what?"

I eventually acquiesced to pick up the pizza - and Ray's impromptu date. Around 6:15 that evening, I headed to the pizza parlor to pick up the pie Ray ordered minutes earlier. I walked up to the takeout counter.

"Hi. Excuse me," I said to the short man behind the glass. "Is my order ready? It wa called in for Ashley Jay."

"What was your order?" He asked through a heavy Mexican accent.

"A large chicken and broccoli pizza," I replied. He handed me a piece of paper with the number scribbled on it.

"Take a seat," He said and pointed toward the bar stools. I pulled out my phone to browse the Internet to kill time. As I am scrolling, I spotted

Chris huddled in a corner booth with a woman and a school-aged boy. I was in direct eyesight of their table but they didn't see me so I hid behind the menu and spied.

I watched as Chris laughed and joked with them. Chris looked very comfortable with them as he patted the little boy on the head. I squinted to make out who he was with. The woman looked familiar. I couldn't make out her face. Her back was turned to me. I could only view her profile but she reminded me of his ex, Austynn. I quickly dismissed the thought.

Chris wouldn't disrespect Taylor like this, I thought as I continued to spy. They exchanged envelopes. The woman opened hers and read from the letter inside. She smiled and slid the paper across the table surface to Chris. Chris put his head down. Chris's hand shook as he attempted read the paper she had given him. Chris kept his head down, unable to read it.

He ripped open his envelope but didn't read that one either. He handed them both to the woman. She urged him to read it. She waved the paper in his face and pointed. Chris started sobbing but with a smile on his face.

"Number 44," the man behind the counter yelled. "A large chicken and broccoli pizza," he shouted. "Number 44. Ashley Jay," he said. *Damn it! He's going to blow my cover.* I jumped up and beelined toward the counter. The man handed me the pie and as I handed him my credit card. I could see Chris walking over to me out the corner of my eye.

"Ashley Jay," Chris said nervously as he stood up against the counter.

"Christopher," I mocked his tone. "What are you doing here?"

"It's pizza night for everyone, it seems," Chris suggested. He laughed as he looked over his shoulder.

"Let's not pretend that I didn't just see what I just saw. Does Taylor know you're here?" I whispered. The man handed back my credit card and a receipt. I pulled some napkins from the dispenser as I awaited Chris's response.

"No. She doesn't. And I'm hoping you could keep this between us," he said with a straight face.

"What exactly am I keeping between us? Because it looks like you're on a date?" When Chris maintained his silence, I continued. "And who is that woman? From here, she looks a lot like Austynn," I said as I looked at him with confusion. Still no verbal response from him.

His non-verbals were blaring his guilt. He bowed his head, paced back and forth and rubbed the back of his neck.

"Chris! You have got to be kidding me," I said. "You out here having dinner with her?"

"It's not like that Ashley Jay, I swear," Chris lamented.

"But that is her," I asked, which he affirmed with a simple head nod. "Is there a good reason why you're here with her? Of all people Christopher, really?! Do you want Taylor to kill you?"

"It's really not what it looks like," Chris said.

"Well...I don't know what you think it looks like from your view, but mine was very clear. And clearly something's going on."

"It's a long story," Chris said.

"How about you start at the beginning," I said sternly with my arms folded. Chris paced the small space between us and glanced back at Austynn and the boy. Chris grabbed the nape of his neck, sighed heavily and turned back to me.

"Taylor would seriously kill the both of you," I said. "Why would you come out in such a public place with a whole 'nother family?"

"What are you doing here?" Chris said. "Are you picking up something?"

"Did you just happen to run into her or was this a planned event? This is none of my business. I'm about to call Taylor." I pulled my phone out of my handbag and began to walk away from the counter. Chris snatched my phone from my ear. I just stood in the middle of the doorway, stunned idle.

"I'm going to hold on to this. Let me walk you to your car," Chris said as he held the door open for me as I reluctantly walked through.

"Taylor kept saying you were up to your old ways. I just couldn't believe it. I kept defending you. And it turns out she was right," I mumbled as I stomped toward my car.

"It's not what you think. I just need you to look out right now. I know it doesn't make sense, but I promise it will," Chris pleaded. "As long as you promise me you won't tell Taylor."

"I can't promise you that. I can promise you that I won't let you hurt my best friend again. I promise you that," I said as I got into my car.

"I just found out some news. And I need a little time figure out how to explain things to Taylor. I can't have you telling her what you saw and having her think it's more than it is. Please," he pleaded.

"What kind of news warrants dinner with your favorite ex and her child?"

"Just know, I'm not out here cheating on my wife," Chris said. "I came here to find out..." Chris paused. I could tell he was hesitant to divulge too much. Yet there was an excitement in his eyes that said he wanted to tell me more. He paced the empty parking space next to us. "I am the father of Austynn's son Kristian," he blurted out with a huge grin. My eyes widened. I put one hand over my mouth, let out a silent scream and pushed him with my free hand.

"Shut up! You're lying. Did you just say you're Kristian's father? The same Kristian that Taylor asked you about seven years ago when Austynn was pregnant? That Kristian? Are you trying to get *me* killed?"

"I know it's a lot to hear. It's a lot to say! I didn't lie to Taylor. I also didn't know then what I know now. So can you please not tell Taylor about this?"

"What? That just gives me even more reason. How do you know that's your son? Is that what's in those letters you two were passing back and forth?"

"Oh, you saw that too," he said wiping his forehead.

"I saw everything, Chris!" I shouted. "You need to take a test to be 100% sure. You can't just take her word for it," I blurted out in a panicked breath. "Taylor is going to kill you! Does Austynn's husband know?"

"Yes, and that's not her husband, anymore, they are divorced," Chris answered.

"Convenient," I countered.

"Ashley, listen, I know you mean well, but this really isn't any of your business. And I got this. I just need to know that you won't tell Taylor before I do. I swear I will tell her. I just have to figure out how. Please," Chris pleaded with me.

"I can't even...have you lost your mind? That's my best friend, she's like a sister and you got her out here looking more foolish than Ashanti! And you're asking me not to tell her? What's wrong with you?"

"Again...I just need some time to tell her myself. And with all due respect, this is a family matter."

"Wow, so I'm not family now? You get a brand new kid and you start acting brand new, I see. But you want me to keep your secret from my best friend?!" I panted through squinted eyes, fighting back tears. I stared at Chris in utter disbelief. In the blink of an eye, a stranger stood in front of me.

"Don't take it like that. Please," Chris reprieved. "I didn't mean it that way."

"Listen. You're right. This is none of my business," I said, dismissing his sudden sorrow. "I can't promise you I won't tell Taylor but I will give you some time."

100

"Thank you Ashley," Chris said, relieved. "I knew I could count on you," he said smiling as he reached for a hug.

"Don't thank me now. Because, honest to God on your life, I will make it my business to put you on blast if you don't tell Taylor. And soon! Now give me my phone back so I can leave," I said as I held my hand out.

"Some men never change," I said as I snatched my phone from Chris when he handed it to me then slammed my car door enough to rattle the inside. My heart felt heavy with disappointment for Chris's sudden audacity and boldness.

Ray
Got Til It's Gone

"Don't it always seem to go that you don't know what you've got 'til it's gone?" - Janet Jackson

I hopped into the front seat of Jade's car. I waited for a reply from Ashley, who was taking longer than usual to respond. "Thanks for the ride little bro," I said as I looked at my watch then checked my cell phone again.

"No problem," Richie said. "You going to be home later?"

"I may be. It depends on how mad Ashley is," I responded.

"I'm surprised she's letting you come back around," Richie said.

"When will you overstand that we have a special effect on the ladies? At least, I do, little bro," I said. "Ashley could never stay mad at me."

"Jade would kill me if I stay away from her for an 8-hour shift. You be gone from your girl for too long."

"The last four days doesn't count. Besides it's for the best. Do you really think Ashley can handle being exposed to the binge episodes of Shirley King?"

"We can barely handle them," little Richie said.

"Exactly my point," I argued.

"But you can't disappear every time Shirley binges. That's Shirley's life. You taught me that. If she's not willing to live for her kids...her kids can't do anything about how she chooses to live."

"Easy for you to say. You never had to do this with her..."

"No. So, stop trying to save her," Richie said. "Is your name Jesus? She's not going to do anything but resent you. In the meantime, you're eopardizing your future because your mother can't stop chasing her past."

"You're way too insightful to only be 18," I noted.

"Age ain't nothing but a number, Ray," Richie replied as he pulled up to Ashley's waterfront condo. "You have to learn when to let it go, big brother."

"I'll hit you up later if I need a ride," I said to my little brother.

"Ok. Cool. Peace bro," he said as he pulled off. I still hadn't receive any messages from Ashley so I used the key she gave me and let myself into the house. I slid on my #FlySlides and plopped on the royal blue sofa in the living room. I stared out the baywindow at the small waves crashing against the shore and waited for Ashley to arrive with the pizza. I texted Ashley to let her know that I was here.

"What's up baby? How's everything?" Ashley said as she walked through the front door moments later. I grabbed the pizza box from her hands and placed it in the middle of the coffee table. I went into the kitchen to grabbed three plates, hoping she wouldn't bring up the last week. I came back into the living room and noticed Isaiah wasn't tagging behind her as usual.

"Everything is good. Where's Isaiah?" I asked as I plated two slices for Ashley.

"That lucky little guy is going to Paris for a week with the grands," Ashley said. I bit into a slice of pizza. "What about you? Where have you been? It's been five days."

"I've been busy," I said without looking up from my plate of carbs.

"With what?"

"Work. Family. Wedding planning."

"Wedding planning? You missed appointments we've had scheduled for months. What's really going on?" Ashley picked pieces off her pizza slice and nibbled at them like a bird pecking for seeds.

103

"I haven't slept in four days. I've been on the hunt for Shirley. She's binging again."

"You don't have to lie on your mother," Ashley said.

"I'm not lying. Why haven't you gotten up with your girls?" Ashley chuckled.

"What's so funny?" I asked.

"It's funny that you would even notice that...that's all," Ashley said sarcastically.

"So you're going to start an argument with me after not seeing me for a couple of days?" I countered.

"I'm not starting an argument. I'm just saying...You realize something about someone and it's the same thing you're guilty of..."

"It's not like that at all. I was simply conversing."

"Ok. So let's converse about why I haven't seen you since I opened up to you about my past? Did I scare you away?"

"Do you think I'd be here now if it did? There is more to life than your insecurities."

"What's that supposed to mean? What am I insecure about?"

"I'm just saying I wasn't around for my own reasons and it has nothing to do with you or what you told me. So don't think that," I empathized.

"How could I not equate your absence to what I told you?"

"I hate to break it to you, baby. Life doesn't revolve around you," I said as I finished the last bite of my slice of pizza.

"Thank you for that unnecessary life lesson. But if that's not the reason then why have you been avoiding me?"

"Why can't you just say you missed me?"

"I would have if I that's what I wanted to say. I am trying to understand you. I've gotten used to our little routine and it kind of vanished when I opened up to you. So this really isn't about life revolving around me - it's about not being able to contact my partner in life for days. You were ignoring me. That's what I'm peeved about."

"Maybe there are some things about my life that I'm not ready to share with you. Have you thought about that?" I asked.

"Well...I hate to break it to you," Ashley said, "but you're not getting rid of me that easily. We're in this together -- and that means you may not be ready to share them with me now but when you are, I'll be here." I couldn't help but digress. Ashley was more mature than most women. She thought logically and answered accordingly. It was the sexiest thing I've ever experienced.

"It's nice to finally spend some time with you," I said. "I've been a little distant for two reasons. And one of them is Shirley.

"What's wrong with Shirley? I thought she doing better since she's been back."

"Well, I thought she was doing better too. Every year Shirley binges around this time, Shirley goes on a binge.

"Why around this time?"

"Big Rich's birthday is coming up and the anniversary of his death is right after that...I just didn't want you to have to deal with all of that. You don't need to see that side of my life."

"I'm not going anywhere, Ray. I could've helped you through that," Ashley said sincerely. I nodded but didn't make eye contact. "I'm here for you through all of it."

"What if I don't want you to be?"

"I mean...if that's how you feel." She shrugged.

"It's just...me and the twins can barely deal with Shirley and her antics - and she's our mother!" I said to soften my last blow.

"Maybe that's why my help can be more effective," Ashley pushed. "I'm indifferent to your situation. Don't try to shut me out of this. I've been here for you since day one. I'm here to help."

"It's too deep," I said as I helped Ashley clean up the living room. We headed to the bedroom once the dishes were cleaned and the trash was taken out.

"Ok. But how long have I known about Shirley? I'm not convinced that's the reason why you've been avoiding me. What's the other reason?"

"I told you there's something else...and this one might change your mind about everything..."

"What else is going on Ray?"

"Listen. My hands were tied. I had no choice."Ashley looked confused all of a sudden. "I don't really know how else to say this but...I lost my job. I feel like I should've told you when it happened but I guess I was embarrassed," I finally admitted.

"But I just saw your pay stubs. You were supposed have went to an event the last time we spoke. It was all lies? Where were you? Whose pay stubs were those you were just flashing around?"

"I know you have a lot of questions. It's a long story."

"Everybody and their long stories today!" Ashley said in a huff. I could see tears beginning to fill up her eyes. "When did this happen?" I took a deep breath and rubbed my forehead.

 "Manny let me go when we got back from the Vegas trip," I whispered. I glanced at Ashley who took a quick trip through her memory to put it all together.

"But...that was in February," she said. She looked up to the ceiling. "It's damn near July. Ray, are you serious? You've been lying to me for the last six months?"

"I have and I'm sorry. I shouldn't have put on a charade. I just didn't want to start off on the wrong foot, telling lies and hiding things. Knowing all that you've been through, that's not my style. Well, not with you."

"Now you're a gentleman now?" Ashley asked. I nodded with reluctance. "Abruptly telling someone you're supposed to care about you've been lying for months isn't exactly a gesture of gentlemen style. Where were you when you told me you were at work?"

"It wasn't like I was sneaking off to go be with some girl. I would go to the station to try and get my job back. I'd try booking meetings with Manny but they'd always get rescheduled. Nothing worked. So I tried getting Mikey's stubs to buy me some more time with you until I finally met with Manny."

"I'm not surprised that you were lying. I'm taken aback by what you were lying about. I was ready for a female hiding in the woodworks but keeping the fact that you no longer have a job when we're planning a wedding is not at all what I expected to hear. It's a bit too much to digest."

"Ashley, I swear that's all it was. I haven't been lying about where I was - I just wasn't getting paid like you thought I was." I hoped Ashley wasn't ready to give up on me and the entire idea of this relationship until I realized she hasn't been completely honest with me either.

"Do we need to call off the wedding?"

"Do you want to call of the wedding?" I asked. I had to look away, somewhat fearful of her answer.

"As far as the money for everything," she asked.

"No. We're good. Deposits have already been made. I still have some of the inheritance money left," I fibbed.

"Are you sure there isn't anything else you failed to share with me?"

"No. What about you?" I countered. "We both omitted information that should've been revealed sooner but we both came clean - and neither of us should be punished for being honest," I pleaded. "I apologize. I know I messed up. I get that. Unless I mess up again, I will marry you. I promise I'm going to be the man you need me to be. And I promise you I won't mess up again because I want to marry you Ashley." She sat quietly for a moment, reflecting on the truth I just laid on her.

"No more shenanigans," Ashley said after a heavy sigh. I leaned forward to get a kiss. Ashley leaned back to dodge my attempt. "You're not all the way forgiven yet. I'm still upset. I'm going to take a shower to get my mind off some things."

Ashley walked toward the door. She smiled softly. "And I have to call Isaiah to say goodnight."

"I'll be right here waiting for you, beautiful," I said with a smile.

"Are you ok?" I asked when she returned. Ashley nodded as she climbed into the bed. She tucked herself under the covers and closed her eyes.

"I'm sorry," I said again with a kiss.

"I know," Ashley replied without opening her eyes. I kissed her again.

"I really love you, Ashley," I admitted. "I want to make this work. Do you forgive me?"

"Yeah, I forgive you," Ashley said. "But please just try to be upfront with me from now on. I can handle the truth, no matter how ugly."

"Noted," I said. I gazed at Ashley lustfully. "Can I get a little...you know," I said looking at Prince as he rose to the occasion. I looked back at Ashley with a grin.

"A little what?" Ashley pretended to not know what I alluded to. "So you think you should be rewarded for lying to me?"

"I think I should be rewarded for coming clean," I gloated. I laughed and caressed Ashley's neck with the tip of my nose. Ashley shuddered to each touch. I kissed my cheek and flashed the infamous dimples.

"You know I'm a sucker for those deep dimples," Ashley said.

"I know. You and everyone else," I said.

"Don't get cocky."

"You know I can't help what God blessed me with," I said as Prince emerged through the slit of my boxer briefs.

"Well, I can see someone's not shy," Ashley said sarcastically.

"Not shy at all. Prince has a mind of his own. You're gonna have to talk to him," I said with a smirk, hoping she'd fall for it. Ashley leaned in. I could feel her breath on the tip. She gripped Prince in her palm and devoured him like a popsicle before I could blink twice.

"Oh my God!" I yelled out as Prince disappeared deep down her throat. Three slurps later my toes curled, fists clenched the bedsheets and my eyes rolled back to a glimpse of heaven.

"Damn, girl. You've been holding out on the King," I complimented as I caressed through her curly tresses. "That's what I've been missing. Let me repay you with some of my own tongue action." I gently pushed Ashley back onto the bed and began to massage her skin with my tongue. She tensed up. I told her to relax.

"Wait, I'm not ready," Ashley said.

"Let me get you ready," I said as I caressed her thick thighs.

"I really do not want to," Ashley said as she curled into fetal position. "I have to take advantage of Isaiah being away. Since you're not working, I'll work some overtime to get our money up," she said. "My dream wedding won't stop because you wanted to keep your unemployment a secret."

"If you insist, queen," I said. "I just wanted to return the favor."

"I only did it to show you what's to come. And to, hopefully, stop all the begging," she said.

"After that show, baby, you're going to have me begging for something else," I said with a laugh. Ashley giggled.

"I need some rest and so do you," Ashley said. "You don't have to leave when I go to work but you should start looking for a new job."

"Yes, but I also have to look for Shirley," I reminded my future wife. Ashley sighed and rolled over.

"You're using her as an excuse," Ashley said.

"Go to sleep," I said.

When I woke up the next morning, Ashley had already gone into work. I walked into the kitchen and noticed a spatula on the stovetop next to a frying pan on the eye. I checked the microwave. *Jackpot!* She left an egg white omelette in the microwave for me.

 I quickly gobbled the omelette before I took a quick shower. I sent Mickey a text to see what he was up to. He was in with Kennedy so I hit up Richie to see where he was and he was with Jade. RIchie was on his way to work but promised to pick me up to go home after his shift.

"I get off at two this afternoon," Richie said.

"That's too long. It's ten o'clock in the morning. I'll call Shelley." I dialed Shelley's number.

"Bro, you need to get yourself together," Shelley said when I asked her about a
ride. "You can't always depend on us. You need to depend on yourself."

"Shelley when did you become the oldest? All I need you to do is come get me. If it wasn't for me, you wouldn't be thriving like you are."

"You're just going to take the credit for all the work Ashley did for us?"

"I am the reason Ashley is in our lives," I noted. "You should be thanking me."

"Ray, I really wish Ashley wasn't stuck on stupid for you. She really needs to wise up. She's not getting a prize, at all. Y'all don't match. You're a jester and she's royalty."

"You would say that. Just come and get me." Shelley showed up thirty minutes later and dropped me off at the house we grew up in. "I'm headed to Zumba," she said as I got out of the car.

"You need to stop eating Wendy's & McDonald's for that to actually kick in," I said as I chuckled and shook my head. "Has Shirley been home?"

"You are the only one checking for her, Ray. Our mother has been addicted to the street life my whole life. She's an addict. You already know she's in the streets." I search for a sign that Shirley has been in the house. There weren't any spoons missing. No duffle bags randomly thrown by the couch. No half-eaten food on the table or any open drawers and cabinets that were scuttled through. No signs of Shirley in the house at all. I texted a few people and did my normal walk through the neighborhood to see if she was at any of her old hangout spots. No one has seen her. Even Joey couldn't vouch for her whereabouts. How could Shirley just disappear on us again?

The weeks flew by and still no Shirley. Ashley has been too exhausted to spend any time together. Frankly, her excuses were getting old and tired. My normal solution for dealing with my troubles was sex. And ever since I've been with Ashley, Prince wasn't getting the attention he craved. And that's not something I was about to get used to.

"Now who's the one missing in action?" I said when I called Ashley during her break.

"I've added two extra shifts to my three twelves," Ashley said when I asked her on a date. "Why don't you come by the ER and take me to lunch?"

"Lunch wasn't on the menu for what I had in mind," I said cryptically. Ashley usually picked up on my sexual innuendos easily but didn't respond this time. "But seriously. It's been a week since I last saw you. Should I be worried or should I start looking for your replacement?" When she didn't respond with her usual 'try-it-and-see' rant, I knew she was distracted. "I thought you were on break," I said after she answered two different people about e-prescribing medications and wound packing.

"I am, but I'm not," Ashley said. "It's a work thing. You wouldn't understand."

"Where's your son?"

"Isaiah is still in Paris. He'll be back in August just in time for his birthday. Mr. Jax extended his Paris trip for the remainder of the summer. I swear that kid is lucky. He'll be so cultured."

"You're making him act like white people."

"No. I'm making him into a regular child who needs exposure to different cultures to understand the world."

"Sounds about white," I snarked.

"You're so funny," Ashley said dryly. "You can come by later if you want. But I have to go back in at midnight."

"Ashley, you're at work now. You can't seriously be working this much for the wedding."

"I've been planning this wedding for six and a half months now, but really it's been a plan in my head since I was a little girl. I waited for this wedding my entire life and I will not allow your unemployment to downgrade my dream wedding decor."

"All I hear is a lot of Is, mines and mes."

`

"Ray, I have to go," Ashley said perturbed. "There's blood everywhere. I'll call you back!" Ashley said.

"Promise," I asked.

"Yes, oh no. I promise. Dammit it needs a tourniquet," she screamed before hanging up the call. *I need to find a job*, I thought. I can't have my wifey out her working this hard. *It makes me look bad. But what can I do? Being that my only skills are basketball and sex.*

"Ashley would kill me and hide my body before she's done calling off the wedding, if I went back to my old ways," I thought aloud. "It would be so easy," I said as I scrolled through unanswered messages and requests from old friends and recent exes.

Later in the week, Ashley finally had a break in her schedule to spend some time loving on her man. I had Shelley cook up her famous seafood mac and cheese to surprise Ashley with. I borrowed Shelley's car for the night since she didn't have to go back to campus for her two college-prep courses.

Ashley was still in her scrubs when I got to her house. Even though we hadn't seen each other in almost two weeks, Ashley and I didn't miss a beat. She was still as beautiful as I remember her. I kissed her hello and put the casserole dish on the dining room. Ashley changed into NOIR boy shorts and tank top. She sat down at the table and smiled at the plate I served her.

"With all of this overtime, I'll be able to keep us afloat. At least until you secure something," Ashley said as she munched on her food. She scattered the fork through the noodles, picking out the shrimp.

"We don't need a fancy wedding, Ashley," I reminded her. "We can just go to the justice of the peace." She looked up from her food in disgust.

"I wish I would. I can not accept that. If that means I'm paying the remaining balances by myself - then so be it." Ashley tilted her head back and laughed. "Justice of the peace" she repeated and laughed again. "Good one," she said as she stuffed a forkful of shrimp into her mouth.

"That means our time together will be cut even shorter than it is now."

"I don't see how that's a problem, considering, you made it this way. Keeping your unemployment a secret was a choice - in my 'Ye voice." Ashley snided. "I will not sacrifice my dream wedding because of your omission."

"Whatever you say," I digressed. "I hope you love sex as much as you love planning this wedding."

"Ugh. All you talk about is sex. Yet all I do is work." Ashley said. "How unattractive is that?"

"You don't have to work as much as you do," I argued. "We went from loving to understanding to this. I see you whenever you're available, which isn't much."

"It won't be like this for much longer, Ray," Ashley said with a mouthful. "It's not as serious as you're trying to make it."

"Doing all the working that you're doing is a choice...your choice," I said. "In your 'Ye voice. And almost all of the deposits have been paid."

"Deposits have been paid but balances are still due. And we still have to book the band, find footwear and decide on party favors.

"There's still so much to do. The hotel is booked but we have a $1500 balance left to pay by October. And our Parisian honeymoon experience still has to be paid for."

"That gives us about what...three to four more months to pay it," I said nervously as I counted on my fingers. "And they are really making sure they get their money. Months before the wedding day...That's a hustle."

"We also have to give the band our song list and what else?" Ashley tapped her forefinger against her chin. "Oh did you make the reservation for the Lamborghini drop top?"

"I thought you were handling that, too" I said.

"I can't do everything, baby."

"Even if you do everything so well?"

"Flattery gets you nowhere in wedding preparations, babe." I shrugged. "It was a nice try though," she said with her gorgeous smile. "I thought so," I said as I leaned in to kiss my beautiful fiancé.

"How are you going to do it all if you're working?"

"That where you come in fiancée."

"I feel like that means trouble and requests I won't be able to deliver on."

"You're full of free time so it shouldn't be a problem."

"What do you need me to do?

"I need you to go to the crafts store for the ribbon & wooden pallet boards."

"That sounds like a lot of woman work. Are you sure you need me to handle this?"

"Yes. Unless you want to put a splint on a broken finger."

"I'll let you tend to the nursing duties."

"For you, I'll do anything." I leaned over to give Ashley a kiss. She gave me her cheek.

"Except work apparently," Ashley said, now offering her lips.

"Touche," I said. "I'll pick up whatever you need. Just text me the details."

Over the next few weeks I ran all of the pre-wedding errands like I was Ashley's hired help. From paying the officiant to mailing out our save the date cards, I did it all and everything in between. Even though I tried to keep the peace, my weariness began to show.

"Ok," Ashley said as soon as she sat into the passenger seat of her car. "Did you get my list of things to do done?"

"Well, damn! Hello to you, too," I said as I blew a kiss into the air.

"I apologize, babe," Ashley said as leaned in to kiss my cheek. "I had to make sure."

"You should make sure you greet your man, first. Ask him if he ate. Show a little more concern, but yes, I got everything done on your list." Ashley squealed in excitement as she clapped her hands together.

"Did you decide if you wanted the Mr. & Mrs. cake topper or a crown?"

"You know I want the crown," I said. "It's only right!"

"Ok. Then that can be your task tomorrow. You can pick up the crown from Michael's with the rest of the party favors."

"Oh ok. Guests get crowns too," I said with a smile. "Wait, how much are they?"

"You said the crowns cost too much when we discussed it earlier so we are going with cookies with crowns on them."

"Cookies? That's lame. When did we decide that?"

"When Miss Amy said she would bake at no charge."

"Well...I love cookies, then, especially if they're free!"

"I'm still waiting on flights for our honeymoon to go down there. Right now, they're at $1,300-$1,500 round trip, non-stop. I'd rather pay around $1,100 but that's only for connecting flights." Ashley babbled on for another ten minutes about stuff I didn't care about. Women-stuff. Details. I responded to her with mhmms and sounds like a plan.

"Great. You'll do it tomorrow?" Even though I agreed I was definitely unsure of what I just volunteered to do.

The next morning, I awakened to an empty bed. Ashley left another list on the bedside table with her VISA credit card beside it. I reached out to Shelley.

"I need to borrow your car again," I said to my younger sister.

"I need you to get your own car, big bro," Shelley responded. "I need to go to work."

"Cool," I said. "I will drop you off. I should be done with these wedding plans before you're out of work. You can drop me at Ashley's later."

116

At Jerry's Artarama, I sifted through Ashley's detailed list. As I perused the aisles, I noticed a big booty bent over on the floor. She reached to grab something from the bottom shelf.

"Pull over that ass is too fat," I sang aloud as I passed the girl on her knees.

"Raymond King," a familiar voice called out. "Fancy seeing you at a craft store."

"Alana," I said as I cringed on the inside when I heard her voice. "What are you doing here? Stalking me, I see?"

"Don't flatter yourself, Ray," Alana said. "I'm not a stalker. I'm here to pick up some things for a party I'm having in a few months."

"You need me to make an appearance at your party?"

"Ugh. Your nerve is as big as your ego." Her annoyance began to show with all the eye rolling, crossed arms and dismissive hand gestures. "I've been trying to reach out but you're in a situation," she said with hand quotes. "So I had to go about it differently."

"I'm getting married. That's not a situation."

"I know. I'm just trying to show respect," Alana said as she grazed her body against me.

"That position reminds me of something else you used to do."

"Please don't remind me," Alana said with an attitude.

"What's up?" I asked. "We should really get together."

"I'm not available to hang out. I'm working at Harry's tonight."

"I can stop by and get a drink or two. You can feed a king," I said.

"You're always looking for a come up," Alana said as she waddled through the store. "I really need to pee." The memory of Alana's wetness flashed through my mind.

117

"That sounds familiar," I insinuated. I smiled a suggestive grin. Alana would always say that after our sex sessions.

"What happened to Mr. Engaged? Keep all that energy that you been had," Alana said as she dodged my advances like a goalie.

"For someone who was so adamant so see me sure is acting a lil' different now that I'm here," I said softly in her ear.

"Listen Ray, we're cool and we will always be cool but you're getting married and I'm..."

"You're going to see me later and you can finally expose what you've been dying to tell me."

"I don't think you're ready to hear it but ok," Alana said "I'll see you later."
Alana walked away. I spotted the party favor boxes Ashley had ordered and checked the bins for the red ribbon. After two hours of errand running for Ashley, I received a reminder text message from Alana about our meeting later.

"Don't forget," the message said and included a photo incentive to make sure I came.

Later that night, Ashley came home from work exhausted. She sat at the edge of the bed. She removed her Crocs and started to rub her feet.

"I need another shift," Ashley said as she undressed. With only a lace thong and a see-through bra on, she fell back on the bed and sighed before she snatched the remote out of my hand. Ashley angrily flipped through channels. She mumbled at every commercial and huffed at every sitcom joke. I tried to calm her down by being her personal butler.

"I'm going in the kitchen. Do you want anything," I asked.

"Water," she said. I fetched her a cold bottle of water.

"I need ice," she said after gripping the bottle. "It's not cold enough and I don't drink straight from the bottle." I ran back to the kitchen to grab Ashley a glass filled with ice cubes. "It's not ladylike," Ashley said as she poured water from the bottle into her glass. A droplet fell on her exposed thigh and I wiped it off.

"Next time," I said. "I'll show you what my mouth do." I flickered my tongue, grinning.

"Please don't," Ashley said with an attitude.

"You don't know what you're missing," I said with a wink. "You need a shower anyway, you're salty."

"Well, you need a job, but you don't hear me complaining," she said.

"Oh, I hear it. It's just smothered in sarcasm," I said. She rolled her eye and sulked for a moment. She stretched as she walked into the closet. Ashley pulled out a pair of yoga pant and polka dot tank top and went into the bathroom to run a bath. Forty-five minutes later Ashley re-emerged looking bright faced and calm. I rubbed her shoulders and kissed her neck.

"You just need some dick," I whispered. "It'll relieve all that stress."

"Ugh. Here we go again. How are you not tired of bringing it up? I am cel-i-bate."

"Celibacy is boring. You don't think it's beyond crazy that you want to marry me but you don't want to have sex with me?"

"I do want to have sex with you. Have you seen you? I'm not dead. It's just..." She hesitated. "I would prefer to wait until we are married. I made myself a promise and if you really love me like you claim, waiting shouldn't be that difficult."

"Why do you always say that? I do love you but there's so much patience a man has. I never met anyone as dedicated as you are to this whole celibacy thing. There has to be more to it than you're telling me. You have like superhero willpower. I never seen anything like it. It's crazy. Don't you want to please your man?" Ray sat behind me and rubbed my shoulders. I stood up and began to pace the room.

119

"I will please you. I swear it will be worth the wait."

"I'm tired of waiting. Another five months is too long. Do you know how much pussy I gave up for you?"

"Do you really expect me to think you gave up all your thirsty thots before I gave you any? I don't look that stupid, do I? I'm sorry if I do because I am not. At all."

"From my seat, you're looking pretty damn dumb because I did. I gave up every single chick that was stuck. STUCK! They would do anything for me kind of stuck, like please me with a little surprise head here and there or some ass whenever I wanted. Maybe I should go back to my old ways. I stayed winning back then."

"You can't be serious," Ashley proclaimed. At that very moment, for the first time since we met, my feelings for Ashley began to attenuate. "If that's where you're going to take this, maybe you shouldn't sleep here tonight. If it's going to be a problem that causes us to argue, I'd rather you go home and get your feelings out. At the end of everything, you knew what it was when you got involved."

"Yeah, you were single and celibate. Now you got a fiance and your man got needs."

"So what do you want me to do when this relationship, this engagement was all your idea? How do you beg someone to be with you only to find out it's work to get me? You've been telling me you wanted to be my husband since we met. Now it's 'a man's got needs.' What else do you want from me?"

"Some pussy would be nice. But I'll take what I can get. My dick has a mind of its own. What you're not willing to do, someone else is."

"Well maybe you should call whoever else is willing," Ashley said. "I am not into all the pushing you're doing, considering you literally knew what you were signing up for: no sex until we're married."

"If I leave and I can't promise you that I'll be back," I said as I gathered my things to make a dramatic exit. Ashley walked up to me and stood in front of me. She placed her hand on my chest as she stared into my eyes and leaned in to whisper into my ear.

"Trust me, you will," Ashley said. "You'll be back. You don't want to lose the bet you have with yourself. You want me. You know you do. And you'll marry me to get what you want. And I want to get married so go have your fun. Get it out of your system. But know like I know you'll be back."

I stood in the doorway, somewhat shocked and reluctant to walk through, unaware of what to expect next. Ashley kissed my cheek and walked away. She dismissed me with a simple hand motion and once she was out of sight, my feet began to move without a second thought.

As soon as I was in the car, I called Alana to see if she made it to work yet. Alana didn't answer. I drove to Harry's and waited in the parking lot until I saw her. I spotted her Mustang park next to a lamp post an hour later. I sat outside for another 15 minutes to allow her time to get on the dining floor.

I walked into the eatery and sat down at a booth. When the waiter approached the table, I ordered two drinks and asked him to summon Alana. I tipped him a five dollar bill and he nodded.

Moments later Alana emerged from the back in a smock apron and a nametag. She placed a napkin on the table and pulled out utensils from her oversized pockets. The waiter returned with two drinks. He placed one drink in front of me and the other across from me.

Alana stared at her favorite drink beside her and frowned. Alana looked around. "I didn't order this," she shouted at the waiter walking away,

"No, but I did," I whispered in the low, erotic voice she was all too familiar with. I smiled to reveal my dimple. "Hello again, Miss Davis." Alana grinned like a child after a surprise visit to Chuck-E-Cheese. "Have a drink," I said pointing to her glass.

"I can't drink while I'm working," Alana said. "What brings you here?"

"You," I said as I downed the drink I ordered for her. "You can watch me drink and tell me your big news."

"How have you been?" Alana asked as I sipped on my second drink. I stared at Alana's bulging cleavage. I made eye contact briefly and licked my lips. I took another sip of the drink and smiled.

"That weight looks good on you," I complimented.

"You don't want to talk. You want to fuck," Alana said. "I can see it in your eyes."

"So. What's wrong with that?"

"What about your lady?" Alana said.

"Didn't we talk about your overwhelming concern for the other women in my life? Worry about yourself."

"Oh, you're testy tonight," Alana said.

"I'm horny," I announced. "And you can always assist with that."

"I don't think I can, actually." She paused. She rolled her eyes before sighing. "I'm pregnant," Alana revealed. She patted her rounder than usual belly.

"I heard pregnant pussy is the wettest," I said with a smile. "You trying to let me see if it's true?"

"Seriously, Ray," Alana said with a stern look in her eyes. She folded her arms across her chest. "That's why I've been looking for you. I've been trying to tell you that I'm pregnant. I'm due in September. You do the math..."

"Whoa. Hold up. Slow down. *You are* the one who's pregnant; why do *I* need to do the math? Why would any of this matter to me at all?"

"If you would let me finish, I could explain," Alana said.

"Nah, explain to your kid's father - not to me. Let's be real about this, La," I said in an anxious pitch. "I thought I would get some food, a little

122

head and maybe some ass but not an unnecessary explanation on how you got pregnant."

"This explanation is for you - and you only," Alana said while she rummaged through her purse. She pulled out ultrasound pictures, visit notes with her due date and a screenshot of her pregnancy test dating back to November of last year. "And you know how. That reverse cowgirl position you love so much."

"This proves nothing," I said as I got up from the booth. "You know I was just trying to smash. I didn't come here for all of this."

"I know. That's why I led you believe that was a possibility. Give me more credit than that...I know you very well. I didn't make you have sex with me then...and I can't help that you're engaged, now," she said with a nonchalant shrug of the shoulders. "You always said you would marry the girl who has your baby...I'm just holding you to it."

Alana knew me better than I knew myself sometimes and she was right about one thing. I couldn't handle this. Not right now.

"Is that what this is about? Because I'm getting married - in five months. And let's not forget that...I don't want to be with you," I said. "I never have."

"You can't run away from your responsibilities forever, Ray," Alana said as she got up from the booth to return to kitchen. "If you're not going to be with me...you will be going on child support."

Taylor
Last Night
"I'm all cried out with nothing to say" - Sean Combs & Keyshia Cole

Another weekend passed as I prepared my clothes for an impromptu mid-morning brunch date with Ashley she invited me to just this morning. Being that we only had two weekends left until the kids came back from Paris, Ashley and I had to squeeze in any kid-free fun we could. And with us both working, there was little time to have private chill time, even with our scheduled Ladies Night. Ashley and I were like sisters, so I cherish the times we are able to hang out, especially when Morgan was Ashley's favorite plus one.

"This is the best place for my vegan palate. I want two vegan pancakes with the roasted sweet potato hash," I said as I quickly examined the menu.

"Since it's my cheat day, I'm getting the New York benedict. I could already taste the sear on my steak," Ashley said as she let out a little grunt. She giggled.

"Aren't you happy our Friday nights at Toca's were replaced by Sunday brunch at Julian's?"

"I know you are," Ashley retorted.

"Mainly because I needed some Ashley time sans Morgan. Ugh, your friend. She has a hood side I cannot deal with," I said as I sipped a Pellegrino water with lemon and lime wedges swirling around my straw.

"You two are very similar," Ashley said.

"That's an insult, Ashley, really. You know I'm way more bougie than I am hood." I waved my hand to move on. "I want every detail about you and Ray. Did you call off the wedding? I'm asking with fifty percent concern - the other fifty, I'm kind of hopeful that you did."

124

"It was postponed." Ashley did not make eye contact.

"Indefinitely?" I said with one eye closed and a slight grin. Ashley rolled her eyes and shrugged.

"We're in limbo, right now. He reaches out but stays away. He said he can't be around me as attracted as he is to me and not have sex. And..."

"Even though he knew what he signed up for. Ray hasn't been back since that day I baited him to leave, besides an 'I miss you' text here and there. That was weeks ago. Taylor, I'm just," Ashley exhaled a long-winded breath.

"I wasn't expecting him to leave yet I wasn't in a position to argue. I know he has needs. I'm sure he'll find somebody thirsty enough to fill those needs. Knowing Ray, any willing participant will do. He always had a stream of flows to choose from."

"That just shows that I was right about Ray all along," I said.

"And that's what sucks the most," Ashley said, sullenly. "I knew to keep my guard up but swore he was different. He showed me something different, you know?"

"It's all for the best. He obviously couldn't handle the commitment he asked you for, which would ultimately dictate how your entire relationship would be." I paused for a second once our food arrived. "Does this mean I can hook you up with Jerome?" I have been trying to convince Ashley to drop Ray for some time now.

Even though Ray was cool, I knew he wasn't for Ashley. Her stories about him weren't always in his favor, but he never redeemed himself. I've been telling Ashley about Jerome for weeks now. She didn't share my sentiments but Ashley let her emotions guide her decisions when logic should. Jerome was more her cup of tea.

"Jerome is an accountant. He worked for Delta as a junior-level accountant executive. He drives a new Acura and owns a waterfront two-bedroom condo, just like you do. He relocated to Providence to work for Daddy around the same time I started. I just think you and him would hit it off," I enthused.

125

"He sounds more like your type than mine," Ashley said. "Maybe you should date him."

"I'll pretend I didn't hear that. Even on my worse day, I'll ride for Chris."

"Speaking of Chris, how's that been going?"

"Do not try to change the subject. You can meet Jerome at the next ladies night."

"Ladies night is usually at one of our houses," Ashley said. "And it's supposed to be at my house this time."

"Girl, we are going out! The kids come back the week after next. This time out is long overdue," I persuaded. "And this brunch doesn't count."

"You sound way to excited for this," Ashley noted.

"Wait until you see him and you'll understand," I said.

"This sounds dangerous," Ashley said. "Now can you answer? How are things with you and Chris?"

"Chris has been distant lately. Even though things have been going well between us, I could tell there's something that's keeping him distant from me."

"How so," Ashley said. She sifted around in her chair as if the conversation made her uncomfortable. I could tell she didn't want to pry but her cup was ready for this tea.

"He's been taking longer than usual store runs, coming back with nothing he went for. He claims to be working every Thursday. Those extra shifts never add up to extra money. And, you know, now he can't blame it on my spending habits because I spend my own money - and I still have Daddy's credit card," I said with a wink. "But Chris just leaves too much to the imagination. When I try to talk to him about anything, he gets defensive. You know what that usually means. He's hiding something."

"What if he isn't cheating," Ashley said.

"What if he is back at it, though," I countered. "Either way, I don't want to know yet."

"Why not?"

"Mainly for two reasons, one: I was too busy buried into building a name for myself, doing something I am great at, you know, outside of my father and without my husband's name attached to it. That feels good to have my own. And two: I'm not ready to find out if Chris is still playing games. I've worked too hard on this marriage for it to be a farce. And I'm not ready to leave so whatever he is doing, can be done in peace...for now."

"It isn't all for appearances, is it? You love Chris. So, if you're not happy, it's okay to admit that you're not happy. You have nothing to prove to anyone."

"Ashley...when Chris and I took our marriage vows, we said forever. Thick and thin. Ups and downs. Broke and rich. Not once did we mention happy. We vowed to be life partners through all of life's cycles. And sometimes, life isn't always happy. I'm with Chris through it all and not everyone will understand that."

"The new Jada & Will?" Ashley asked as she laughed out loud. "Life partnership and marriage are the same thing."

"Minus the expectations...You wouldn't understand," I retorted. "You're not married. Marriage isn't for everyone. People do it for the wrong reasons, and usually, those are the marriages that don't last. I just know I married for love. I can only hope Chris did too."

"Fair enough. Just prepare yourself. It might not be anything you expect," Ashley said.

"You sound like you know something," I noted. "What's good?"

"How's work going?" Ashley asked to change the subject again. This time, I allowed it.

"Pretty well, actually. Jerome and I work pretty closely. He's the money guy so I have to run certain salary packages by him to make sure there's budget for it. And we just clicked. Everybody says it, even Daddy. He loves how cohesive his team is."

"That's great. Glad to hear it's working out," Ashley said.

"I couldn't be more proud of myself. I've grown so much, you know. So much for being a little spoiled brat, huh? How's work going for you?" I asked.

"It's a circus most the time. Besides the crazy types of cases that come in, girl, my coworkers are out of their mind. I could write a book! The Chronicles of the ER! I can tell you some stories! From the people I work with to what people do in their spare time that causes their trips to the ER... It's always wild there. Never a dull moment! Speaking of," Ashley said as she received an incoming phone call. She rushed off to a quieter area. "I just got called in," she said as she walked back to the table. The waiter joined her with the bill and we finished brunch with to-go bags in tow.

"Don't forget, next Friday, Ladies Night. I'll text you the location. Wear something nice," I yelled out as I climbed into my SUV. Ashley rolled her eyes, nodded and waved goodbye before we pulled off and drove away in opposite directions.

As I drove home, the blue skies turned to mixed hues of pink and purple as the sun set. My usual Sunday nights consisted of an early dinner with my Dad at the Blackstone, a Disney movie with Kaila after bath time, getting my clothes together for my work week and a scheduled sex date with Chris once Kaila drifts off into dreamland. With Kaila away with my parents and Chris at work, my normal night routine changed. I popped open a bottle of champagne and ran the water to fill the jacuzzi.

While I waited for the bubbles to fill, I pulled out an oversized tweed Gucci jacket and a pair of black tights with blue loafers for my Monday in the office, checked the weather forecast then returned the heavy jacket to the closet. I pulled out an oversized, yellow V-neck Gucci cardigan, and replaced the black tights with a green pair and added a pair of Red Bottoms.

I checked the time on my iPhone X. It was after 9 o'clock. I called Chris. No answer. I turned off the running water and stepped into the jacuzzi. I soaked in the jacuzzi until my skin shriveled underwater and drank two bottles of champagne. I reached for a towel to dry my hands before checking the phone again. It was 11 p.m.

I called Chris again. *Voicemail.* I shrugged off the doubt that began to fester and went to bed. The next morning I woke up to an empty bed. I checked my phone and had a text message from Chris that said he was working later because his relief didn't show up yet. He sent the text a little after midnight. I tossed the phone on the bed and got ready for work.

By 6:30 the next morning, Chris still hadn't made it home. I made myself a bowl of strawberries and blueberries topped with whipped cream for breakfast and toasted two slices of rye bread to take with me to work. I grabbed my briefcase and headed toward the garage when I heard the garage door start to rise.

Chris pulled his Mercedes into the driveway as I started to reverse out of the garage. Chris smiled and waved. I returned his smile with a smirk and head nod before speeding off to work.

"Is this a normal Monday for you?" Jerome asked me as I prepared a Keurig cup of coffee.

"No. My husband didn't come home until this morning," I said with a slight grin as I leaned against the countertop.

"Is that sarcasm? Because I was referring to your outfit," Jerome said. "You should be a model."

"No," I said with a smile. "But thanks for noticing my style."

"How could I not," Jerome said. "You're Gucci down to the tights, girl. Looking runway ready. I see you, girl." Jerome made me laugh any chance he got. He was like my personal cheerleader. I smiled again but remained silent in thought.

"You hide so much behind that smile," Jerome said.

"You have no idea," I said as I perked up.

"Just tell me. You can tell me anything. It's man problems, right? It's always the pretty ones."

"I'd rather be pecked to death by a flock of hummingbirds than talk about Chris right now," I said as I sipped from my coffee mug. Jerome smiled awkwardly. "I thought Chris and I were on the same page but now I know we aren't."

"Did he tell you where he was the other night?" Jerome asked.

"He did. He said he was at work. His regular excuse, especially since I can't complain about him working. I would really like to know what he's up to because I don't think he's being honest."

"Just know...I'm here to help," Jerome said and I liked that. Jerome always extended a helping hand or a listening ear. Yet, despite my feelings toward my husband at the moment, I was committed to our marriage no matter how refreshing Jerome's existence in my life was.

"I appreciate it," I said as I walked out of the break room. "It's really nice to hear but let me get to work." I tried to bury myself in my work projects and sifted through resumes, only to find myself upset at Chris's audacity as of late. What am I missing?

When I got home, Chris was in the kitchen. He had pasta shells spilled across the table, pieces of chicken bits sauteeing in the frying pan as he cut up broccoli stalks. He had a loaf of Italian bread on the counter, sitting next to his favorite spices, oregano, basil and garlic powder.

"Hi baby," he said when I walked past him.

"Hi," I replied dryly. He leaned in for a kiss, which I thwarted. I walked into the bedroom and undressed out of my work clothes into a tank top and shorts.

"Would you like me to make your plate," he asked when I re-emerged.

" No. I would actually like for you to explain yourself. Where were you last night?"

"I let you know where I was," Chris said.

"Do you think that matters? This isn't what I signed up for, you not coming home. This doesn't look good."

"That's your problem. You care what everyone else thinks and you shouldn't. I'm not doing anything wrong."

"Not coming home is wrong, Chris. You're a married man."

"I've been a married man for damn near five years now. And have always acted like one."

"Until last night?"

"Last night was a mistake. There's nothing to explain. It was a mistake. It was nothing more…"

"Ok. It's nothing more to talk about until you're ready to be honest about last night."

"Ok," Chris said and retreated to his mancave to play NFL2K18 and eat his pasta dinner.

Over the next week, Chris reverted back to his old self; love-bombing me with neck kisses and sweet texts; random gifts and surprise lunch dates. He has been getting up a half an hour before my alarm goes off to cook me breakfast, and as I ate, he ironed my clothes for the day.

Chris's surprise lunch dates have become so common - the entire office inquired about what I was going to get - usually before my work day got started.

"What's on the menu today," Jerome asked as he stood in the doorway, a mere ten minutes after I had arrived.

"Chris is sending UberEats. It's Cheesecake Factory," I said. I was buried in paperwork. I didn't look up from my screen.

"He's spoiling you," Jerome said. He began to inch his way into my office.

"Yeah. I know. It's a setup though," I said.

"What do you mean?" He said as he sat down in the brown leather arm chairs in front of my desk.

"He's hiding something and hopes kind gestures will cloud my judgement or at least blind me to what's really going on," I said nonchalantly.

"What do you suspect it is?"

"I can't quite put my finger on it. I just know he's up to something."

"Or maybe he's just spoiling his queen as you so much deserve," Jerome complimented. I blushed. I couldn't help it. Jerome was so random with his compliments and it was refreshing to have someone point out my good qualities instead of finding flaws whenever they got the chance.

"Are you ready for tomorrow night?"

"As ready as every and all professionals are when five o'clock Friday hits," I said, adding a little dance.

"But you're always ready for happy hour," Jerome said.

"This is true," I said.

"Can I join you for lunch today?" Jerome asked.

"I think Chris is supposed to stop by today. He may want to stay around for lunch, he's been all into me lately..." I sighed as Jerome looked on. "We still have tomorrow," I said. "Don't you forget?"

"I like how you just threw me to the side," Jerome joked as he gestured his hand in the air, dismissively. "Yes, we have tomorrow. See you at six."

"See you then," I said as Jerome strolled out of my office. I grabbed my phone to send a reminder text to Ashley. I told her to come an hour later than Jerome and I. As I went scrolled through my call log, I noticed Chris cancelled our lunch plans with the same lame excuse for not coming home every other Thursday: work. I rolled my eyes as I read his message. I simply responded to his text with OK.

Later that night, I came home to an empty house. I prepared for the next day. After a shower and shaving and a snack of sunflower seeds and an orange juice, I nodded off on the couch; secretly awaiting Chris's arrival. I was awakened by a loud boom. Startled, from the explosion that played through speakers of the TV projector, I checked the hall clock. Three a.m. I turned off the television and went into my bedroom. Still no sign of Chris.

Bright and early Friday morning, Chris came home as I left for work. He leaned in for a good morning kiss when I said hello. I dodged his attempt, blew kisses to the air as I passed him and waved goodbye.

"I'm going to dinner with Ashley and Morgan tonight. Right after work," I said quickly. I sat in my car with the driver's door ajar. "I'm actually setting her up with Jerome."

"Setting who up? Morgan?" Chris said, slightly confused.

"I wish I would. Morgan is a cynic. She doesn't need a man - she needs a god."

"I know you're not trying to set Ashley up. She is with Ray. Isn't she?"

"No she isn't," I dismissed quickly. "And it wouldn't matter if she was. Jerome is better," I said. Chris frowned then shook his head.

"Well, have fun," Chris said dryly.

"Thanks," I said. "Just as much fun as you had last night," I slammed the door as I rolled my window up and pulled off.

Co-workers of S. M. Commercial Realty go out for happy hour every other Friday night at Alibi Cafe, guised as the company's after-hour networking event. Usually Jerome and I are the only two in attendance so we became regulars to the Alibi staff.

Jerome and I arrived an hour before I told Ashley and Morgan to meet. We played pool to pass the time. Jerome cracked jokes and talked junk as leaned over the table to aim. I hoped he kept that same energy when I tell him about the blind date I set up for him and Ashley.

After I won the first round, Jerome fetched the first round of drinks as my prize. Jerome then escorted me to our usual table, a poorly lit booth in the back corner, directly across from the bar. I looked over at him as he smiled from the bar.

"Guess what," I said to him as he returned with my favorite drink. Jerome's muscular physique mirrored Taye Diggs during his Stella days.

"What?" he asked as he scooted into the booth, briefly brushing his body against mine. "I got you a Cape Cod made with Ciroc, of course, and ordered fish tacos, southwestern egg rolls and a twenty-piece of sweet chili wings."

"Either you're really hungry or you're already aware I'm having guests," I enthused as I spotted Morgan enter through the glass door.

"Other guests," he said with a grin. His pearly whites shined bright against his chestnut skin as he slid the drink toward my open hand.

"You remember I told you about my best friend, Ashley. She's newly-single and I invited her to meet you." I gazed into Jerome's big brown eyes and poked out my bottom lip. "It was a surprise." Jerome sighed heavily.

"Well, I'm surprised," he said as he gulped a bottleneck beer.

"I think you two will really hit it off," I said sweetly.

"I'll consider it," he said as he leaned in close. "For you," he whispered in my ear. I quivered as his breath braised my neck.

"Well she's here," I said and pointed at the bar where Ashley joined Morgan. Jerome and I walked over to them. I introduced Morgan, first, who simply smiled as she sized him up from head to toe. "And this is Ashley," I said, giving him a slight nudge forward.

"Hi," Jerome said as he extended his hand to Ashley. She reached to give him a firm handshake. He held her hand momentarily before releasing it with a gentle kiss. "It's nice to meet you, finally."

"Hello," Ashley said softly as she forcibly pulled her hand back. "I'm Ashley. And I'm kind of engaged." Jerome chuckled and glanced at me with a smirk.

"Really? That's how you're going to introduce yourself?" I asked Ashley. "You're not really engaged anymore."

"Ashley is an awesome mom and a great nurse. She is kind and generous and low-key funny," Morgan said. Ashley gazed past Jerome as she summoned the bartender to take her order. Jerome tilted his head to maintain eye contact with a disinterested Ashley.

Jerome proceeded with small talk about the warmer than usual weather and traveling throughout the city. As soon as the bartender appeared Ashley quickly turned to order her first two drinks, Hennessy with a splash of Coke.

We all walked back to the booth but I pulled Morgan to me so we could trail behind the new couple I attempted to match-make.

"Morgan, it's your turn to convince her to give Jerome a shot," I whispered as Ashley and Jerome walked three steps ahead of us. Just like a gentleman, Jerome carried Ashley's drinks to the booth. He stood and waited for Morgan and I to get to the table before he sat down. I waved him down so he could sit with Ashley while I talked to Morgan.

"I'm not too sure that would be a good idea, considering it would be a big waste of time. She loves Ray. Let it be."

"Just because you're happily single doesn't mean everyone else should be," I said. "Ashley needs someone like Jerome. He is safe."

"How do you know? You don't even know him," Morgan said as she sat in front of me.

"I know him well enough to know he's a better catch than Ray."

"You don't even know Ray," Morgan said.

"Ugh! You're as useless as the 'ueue' in queue, I swear, why do I even bother with you," I said.

"You're one insult away from starting a war," Morgan said to me. The daggers she threw at me weren't sharp enough to match the look in my eyes. "You can always take your bougie ass home to your sad and empty house."

"My house as full as your mother's stomach after a fifth of good ol' Jack and as happy as she is in front of somebody else's husband," I retorted.

"Ok, ok calm down, both of you," Ashley interjected. "I don't know what's going on but these insults have gone back and forth long enough." Jerome excused himself to answer a call and headed to the bar to check on his food order.

"Now, can we just focus on the reason we're really here? For me! You know that Ray and I put the wedding on hold."

"Was it because of the baby?" Morgan asked.

"What baby?" I asked as I sipped through the skinny red straw of my drink.

"Ray's having a baby with my photography intern," Morgan said. I nearly choked. Ashley rolled her eyes. "It's baby season at my job. Nine women are expecting at the same time. We're going to have back to back maternity leaves. I'm going to be swamped."

"Let's just back up a little bit to the part where you didn't tell me Ray got somebody pregnant," I said, perturbed.

"Ashley forgot to tell her best friend?" Morgan asked me as I glared fire at her. Ashley ignored me as she gazed toward the bottle display behind the bar. After ten seconds she rolled her eyes again and let out a sigh.

"Hmmm. I wonder why," Morgan said. With a smirk, she sipped from her glass and side-eyed me as she put the glass down.

"Because," Ashley said as she gulped the rest of her drink. "We don't know if that's true. Once the baby is born, she'll have a DNA test and we'll be 100% sure."

"Wait a minute," I said. I slammed my drink on the tabletop. "Ashley, you can't be serious," I said. I looked at Morgan. "She can't be serious."

"She is," Morgan responded.

"Beyond serious. This is the man I'm supposed to marry. I have to give him a chance to clear his name. He's not denying the baby, he's just not sure if it's his."

"For real? Ashley is doing what she always does," I said to Morgan, who nodded in agreement. "You're trying to fix it."

"I am not," Ashley retorted.

"Instead of just walking away, you're trying to fix it," I said. "I swear being friends with you drama queens is like having a reality show happen right before my eyes."

"I'm simply being there for my fiancé," Ashley said with a shrug. I rolled my eyes. Ashley finished her first drink and summoned a waiter to order another.

"Well, don't you worry your pretty face. Your *real* best friend has the perfect gift to get your mind off of what's his name," I said as I grabbed her chin and shook it from side to side.

"You mean my future husband?" Ashley asked. "His name is Ray,"

"I mean your soon-to-be-a-thing-of-the-past fiancé," I corrected.

"Well, if my opinion matters,"Morgan interjected. "I think Ray loves you despite what's going on with Alana. I can see it whenever he looks at you. It's undeniable," Morgan gushed. "And to Ray's defense, that Alana chick is low-key crazy. There's some type of imbalance going up up there," Morgan said as she tapped her temple. Ashley and I both looked at her in disbelief.

Morgan expresses the least amount of affect in any situation, especially when it came to love or marriage and she rarely defends men, especially a man with Ray's playboy history.

137

"Maybe he's a really good actor," Ashley said. Morgan and I whiplashed our necks toward Ashley's direction.

"You sound like me," Morgan added.

"I'm shocked," I said with a smirk. "I told you before that your friendship is scary," I reminded. Jerome returned with the waiter trailing behind him with a tray full of food. As Ashley sipped her second drink, I began to formally introduce Jerome to the crew. Ashley began scrolling through her phone.

"I'm engaged, sort of," Ashley blurted out again after a nudge.

"No, she isn't," Morgan interjected. Jerome smiled his shock away. He gulped his drink and chuckled.

"It's complicated. And I'm not ready to date or anything like that yet," Ashley continued.

"I don't want to date either, actually," Jerome said just as I grabbed Ashley and pulled her to the side.

"Ashley Jay Johnson, what in the world is wrong with you? You can't be this infatuated with a man who you haven't even known for longer than you've paid your car note. You already found out he's jobless and lied about it for months. You met him on the verge of homelessness and he may or may not have a baby on the way," I pointed out. "In what state is any of that attractive enough to stick around? At least give Jerome a try. You know I know how to pick them. My track record is impeccable. My sauce is A-1."

"You say that like Chris is Bruce Almighty. Chris is no saint!" Ashley exclaimed. "Trust me."

"Says his favorite cheerleader. Since when do you not stan for Chris? You're worse than the Barbs & the Beyhive for your boy."

"Chris is still a man," Ashley spewed.

"And that means what exactly? It's like you're insinuating something," I said.

"Are you sure he's not the one hiding something? Or does it not matter?"

"Of course it matters," I said. "I don't know what he's doing. I know what he better not be doing." I glanced over my shoulder. Jerome and Morgan laughed as if they were old friends. Ashley and I continued screaming into each other's ears over the DJ's music.

"All I'm saying is Jerome is cool. He's smart. He's funny. He's sexy as hell and I think he's a good match."

"For who? For you?" Ashley asked. She held both my hands and leaned back to look into my eyes for an answer. "It seems like you're the one crushing on Mr. Jerome." I rolled my eyes. Ashley knew me, for sure.

"I'm happily married," I reassured her and myself.

"Girl, please. You're more smitten than a married woman should be over a man you're supposed to be hooking up with your friend."

"You're not worried about Chris like you should be," Morgan added.

"Please, that's insulting coming from you," I pointed out. "You know how much I love Chris. And besides that, Chris is not stupid. I don't need to worry about him."

"Oh, I forgot," Ashley said as if suddenly hit with an epiphany. "You married the only good man left on earth."

"You're in rare form tonight. What's up with all the sarcasm? You love Chris more than I do."

"Correction, I loved Chris's devotion to you and his family. It was a pleasant contradiction to see a man love on you how Chris did. That's what I praised. But he couldn't be perched on a pedestal forever."

"What did he do to you to make him fall from your high graces?" I asked curiously.

"Ask him," Ashley said as she walked back to the booth, leaving me behind with a dumb look on my face.

Morgan and Jerome remained engulfed in their conversation. They didn't seem to notice how long we were gone. "Maybe I'm on your side," Ashley said when I made it to the booth and sat back down.

"Side about what," Morgan asked as she stuffed her mouth with two hot wings and pulled out four naked chicken bones. She giggled in embarrassment before snatching the last wing out of the basket.

"About possibly giving Jerome a chance," I lied.

"I'm good, Taylor," Ashley said. "For real. I need some time."

"I'm right here, ladies. I can hear you," Jerome teased.

"Well, fine. I'm cashing in my I-O-U," I said as I crossed my arms and poked out my lips like a seven-year-old attempting to sass herself into getting her way. "You leave me no choice."

"You can't use an I-owe-you from the tenth grade. It's expired. We're damn near 30."

"Easy for you to say. I saved your ass and you owe me. For life was the deal. So I'm cashing in."

"What happened in the 10th grade?" Jerome asked.

"Taylor saved my ass just like she said. I skipped school to hang out with Eric and I almost got caught."

"Not almost. You got caught, bigtime."

"How?" Jerome asked.

"Ashley's homeroom teacher, spotted her walking down Broadway toward College Hill area going in the opposite direction of school. She told her guidance counselor who called Ashley out the next day and said she was going to call her mother."

"Miss Rita was not going to put me on punishment. That meant no hanging out at the Blackstone. So when she asked for my mom's updated contact information, I gave her Taylor's cell number."

"And when she called, I put on the best impersonation of Miss Rita and saved Ashley's ass from getting suspended."

"Right and since I didn't get suspended I told Taylor I owed her for life," Ashley said as she received her third drink. "But that was literally ages ago."

"And I never cashed it in," I said. "Until now." Ashley rolled her eyes. "I want you happy. And if I can orchestrate some happiness for you... don't fight it, baby girl."

"Gee, thanks for the pitiful handout - no offense, Jerome," Ashley said.

"Be a little more open-minded," Jerome responded. "I could be the reason you won't proceed with your possible wedding vows."

"Someone is more cocky than they need to be," Ashley belted out over the loud music. Ashley's good girl filter dissolved by the end of her third Henny & Coke. "And maybe Chris needs to be more open with you, especially about Austynn," Ashley blurted as she pointed her finger to me. "I tried to tell him to tell you."

"What could Chris possibly tell me about Austynn - of all people?"

"I don't think I should be the one to tell you anything about your man," she said as she swirled the ice cubes around in the glass.

"If it has to do with Chris cheating on me...then yes, you need to tell me, like yesterday."

"I don't think that's what he's doing," Ashley said. "And I don't think I should be the one to tell you what he *is* doing. He said he'd tell you--"

"Some friend you are," I half-joked.

"I'm your best friend, you even said it yourself," Ashley said sternly with a pointed index finger. "But Chris said it was none of my business. That it was a family matter."

"So tell me what you know, best friend," I persuaded. "Because to me, you are family."

"Not according to Chris. He said it was a family matter that I needed to stay out of," Ashley recalled. I wondered what could be Chris's secret be if Austynn was involved and for Ashley to hide it for him.

"I don't feel that way about you and you know that," I pressed.

"You will always be family. Your my nephew's mother. You're my sister from another mister. What family matter would exclude your opinion and include Austynn?"

"That they share DNA," Ashley said as she slurped remnants of Henny, Coke and melted ice, through a red straw.

"What the hell are you talking about? They're related?"

"Noo. It's way deeper than that," Ashley said. I knew Ashley had more to drink than she intended but her revelations made me want to become her personal bartender. I braced myself for an explanation to Chris' recent secretive behavior but wasn't ready for Ashley's big reveal. My heart beat fast as the anticipation grew with every word she uttered.

"I know I shouldn't say anything." Ashley paused. She visibly struggled internally with revealing Chris's secret. She took a deep breath. "Remember when you thought Austynn was pregnant with Chris' baby but he denied it? Then she denied it?" I nodded as I wiped the sweat from my palms. I stared at Ashley while Jerome and Morgan suddenly became silent. Even the R&B music the DJ spun quieted around the room. It was as if time stood still as Ashley spoke on Chris's hidden truth.

"They share a human. They are in fact, Kristian's parents, like you suspected," Ashley finally revealed. "All those years ago!"

"Girl! Stop," I said in disbelief. "Why would he tell you that? And more importantly why wouldn't he tell me?"

"Because he knows his wife," Morgan said. "And you would kill him."

"Chris wanted to wait to tell you," Ashley said.

"Why would he do that?"

142

"He had to figure out how...and if I told you that I saw them together, you would've thought he was cheating with Austynn this whole time."

"When you saw them together? When was this?" I inquired.

"About two months ago," Ashley rambled. "Almost three, now."

"Who did you see, Ashley?" Morgan asked.

"Chris. And Austynn. And Kristian," Ashley slurred. "They were all happy, eating pizza. It was like a family day. That's when Chris found out he was the father. They did a DNA test and everything. He even had papers." I sat silently as I tried to process everything Ashley just dropped on me. Jerome mouthed a question of concern.

"My mascara's too expensive to ruin it by crying. Just know," I said with an awkward smile as tears welled up in my eyes. "I'm feeling a lot of things on the inside." My hands began to tremble as I pulled out my cell phone to dial Chris's number. He didn't answer. I looked around, as a cloud of tears formed in my eyes. I smiled again and ran out before the first teardrop fell. Soon after, Jerome flagged me down.

"You left this at the table," Jerome said. He passed the bag through the cracked window. I began to hyperventilate as I left a message on Chris' voicemail.

"Call me back when you get this," I demanded through the phone.

"Go do what you need to do," Jerome said as he backed away from the car. "I'll take care of the bill. Be safe. And call me when you can."

"Thank you, Jerome. I'll give you a call later," I said as I sped off. I pulled into my garage. I sat in the parked car as I sent Chris a series of heated text messages. He finally responded with a phone call.

"I'm on the way home," he explained. "I had to stop by Mama's house."

"Oh, after midnight? That's strange. But ok. How close are you?"

"Is everything okay?"

"We just really need to talk...like yesterday."

"I'm pulling in now," Chris said before hanging up. I waited with a lit cigarette in the garage, Chris pulled up, ten minutes later, into his side of the garage; left of my Acura truck. Chris hopped out of his new Benz coupe all smiles until he noticed the fizzling cigarette butt on the ground.

"What or who made you this upset? I haven't seen you with a cigarette since before Kaila was born," Chris said.

"You," I said as I lit a second one.

"What did I do?" Chris said, nonchalantly.

"It's what you didn't do that I have an issue with," I said calmly as I inhaled all of the smoke.

"It's not our anniversary."

"No. You didn't forget it this year," I said as I dragged the second cigarette down to the butt within seconds.

"It's not Kaila's birthday."

"No."

"You're not pregnant, right?" Chris asked with a nervous laugh.

"No. I'm actually on my cycle right now," I said as I lit another cigarette.

"Damn, it must be pretty bad. That's three. So, what is it?"

"Where were you last night?"

"Work," he answered. Almost robotically. Chris waved the fog of secondhand smoke out of his face.

"Austynn's house sounds a lot like work in your vernacular," I said. I inhaled the nicotine and exhaled my anxiety.

144

"Austynn? I haven't heard you say her name in years," he said. Chris chuckled like a sociopath caught in a lie. I narrowed my eyes and clenched my fist.

"Yes. Your favorite ex, Austynn."

"Where would you get that idea?" Chris raised his right eyebrow. He paced then rubbed the back of his neck.

"Don't challenge me," I said sternly. His eyes were callous and impassive. I could smack him for how comfortable he was with lying to my face. "Where were you?"

"I just told you where I was. I said work."

"You may have ended up at work, but let's be real. You and I both know you were with Austynn." Chris suddenly got quieter than a church mouse and retreated into the house without another word. I followed behind him.

"Tell me the truth Chris," I nagged.

"Listen," he said. "It's not what you think. It's just that...I am...I have to tell you something that you're not going to like. And I don't know exactly how to tell you, but..." Chris looked at me sullenly then hesitated before looking away.

"You're Kristian's father?!" I blurted out. Chris glared at me then sunk his head. He began to sob. He pulled me into a hug then broke down into tears.

"I'm sorry," he whispered. I pulled back as I fought back the tears that welled up in my eyes. "I'm sorry."

"So..." I paused as I tried to piece the story together. "Ashley wasn't just making up a drunk story?"

"Oh so it was Ashley." Chris punched the countertop. "I told her to wait! I was going to tell you."

"I can't believe you. Why would you keep something like this away from me?"

"Hear me out."

"Why should I listen to you now?"

"I know I should've told you sooner. I didn't really know what to say. I knew you would be upset and take it to another level."

"Upset is an understatement. I'm ready for war. If Austynn even thinks she could get any of our hard earned money because she married a deadbeat..."

"This is exactly what I was trying to avoid. I didn't want you to overreact. Just know that I didn't expect any of this," he said. "I'm just as surprised as you are. Austynn sprung this on both of us."

"No," I said as I shook my head. "You may not have expected it, but you damn sure welcomed it. And excluded me from all of it and we both know why." Chris lowered his head. "You've always wanted Austynn. Yet, she just never chose you."

"Austynn didn't choose me as her child's father; God did. Kristian is mine just like *you* always suspected. It's not my fault I just found out. And for the record, I wasn't trying to hide anything. I just had to figure out *how* to tell you and how to incorporate a new child into the equation as far as spending time and assisting with finances. With Austynn being a single mother now, I didn't...I don't want Kristian to grow up how I did. And I didn't want you to be mad," Chris pleaded.

"You put some thought into this, haven't you?"

"Yes, I have."

"Well I don't know what you were expecting. I won't be a part of this idiocy. Her irresponsibility is not and should not be my problem."

"Why are you being like this?"

"Being like what? Taken aback that my husband, my life partner, my forever," I stressed, "would keep something like this - a whole child - a secret only to find out you told someone else first."

"I look at it like Little Kris is our new child," Chris said with a glimmer of glee.

"Do you want me to leave," I asked as I squinted at the person who stood before me. It couldn't be Chris. Not the Chris that knows me.

"Have you met me?" I asked. "I'm barely interested in Kaila, according to you and your mama, but you want me to accept this new child as my own when you couldn't even mention it to me before you were exposed? I'm starting to wonder who you even are. You obviously didn't consider my feelings in any of this. And what about Kaila? You know, our actual child? Did you think about how this is going to affect her?"

"Kids adjust," Chris said. "She'll get used to it. She's four."

"Regardless, a new sibling is still a lot to adjust to for a 4-year-old, especially when this is the only family she knows."

"A brother is nothing for her to get used to. And besides, she'll love to have a brother. And I thought you would love it, too. I realize keeping it from you wasn't the best move, but one thing I know for sure is, I don't want to lose you over this. I love you, Taylor."

"I'm going to have to disagree. I can see now that you never did."

"I know you're mad, but you know I love you."

"If you did, you would've said something to me and not *my* best friend! And you wouldn't DARE ask her to NOT tell me! That's a violation of our friendship. But you didn't care about the position you put Ashley in, either. It was always about you and how you feel!"

"Please forgive me," Chris begged. "I'm sorry."

"Sorry doesn't fix everything. Were you ever going to tell me on your own? Is that how little you think of me? I can't...I can't forgive you," I said, fighting back tears. I grabbed my car keys and flung my handbag on my shoulder. I stomped toward the door.

"Where are you going? It's two o'clock in the morning. And it's supposed to downpour. Please don't leave."

"Give me one reason why I shouldn't leave," I said with my hand on the doorknob.

"I need you," Chris said. "I love you, Taylor. I'm doing my best here." I looked at him for a moment, silenced to shock. Only for a moment.

"This makes you happy, now, right? You get what you've always wanted...a lifetime connection to Austynn."

"You're saying anything," he said.

"It may not be exactly how you hoped, but..." I shrugged. "It's better than nothing. And what do I get, huh? To share my husband with his favorite ex? Can't you see this ruins everything?" I asked as a single tear fell down the side of my face. Chris didn't respond. He sat silently on the couch as I walked toward the garage door. With that, I walked into the rain without looking back. I drove around the city for an hour before I decided where I should go.

During my ride, Chris called continuously. I did not answer. I couldn't comprehend his callousness when it came to this new dynamic of his relationship with Austynn, He didn't bother to think of how it would affect our everyday lives. I trembled at the thought that I now have to share my husband and the father of my child with someone else. The same someone who he loved at one point. The same someone he wanted to spend his life with at one point.

I felt a pit in my stomach; the life I built was crashing down. I couldn't breathe. My tears blurred my vision; I had to pull over to compose myself.

My emotions paired with the heavy downpour of rain made it hard to think clearly. I pulled into the parking lot of a high-rise that overlooked Diamond Hill reservoir. Without warning, I rang a doorbell and waited. Seconds later, the door opened.

"You look like you need somebody to talk to," a voice said from behind the door.

"I'm glad you answered," I said. "I would've went to my parents but they're still in Paris."

"It's fine. Please come in. I'm happy I could be of assistance."

"It smells like freshly baked cookies and clean laundry. Your home is so clean."

"Shouldn't it be?"

"Well, yes, but it's three in the morning."

"I have the privilege of having you as a guest," Jerome said as he led me into his two-bedroom condo. The thunder rumbled so loud I jumped into the house from outside. I removed my wet hoodie and handed it to Jerome. He hung it up in a closet behind the door and guided me further into his home.

"So, not that I mind, but what brings you here at this hour? Trouble in paradise?" I nodded, holding back tears. "Did you confront him yet?" Jerome asked as he prepared us drinks from his mini bar.

"You know he wasn't even home when I called him after I left you guys at Alibi? He was probably with Austynn and their kid. Making up for lost time." I shook my head in disappointment.

I swallowed the knot in my throat as my lip trembled, then let out a deep breath. "It's crazy. It's always been her, you know? She was always the one he would be with if she wanted him in that way. I was just his default."

"Maybe he chose you because you gave him what he wanted her to give him. You possessed the qualities he looked for in a wife," Jerome reasoned. "You are a gem, you know?"

"Well..." I said as I thought back. "That wasn't too hard. I was his first something, you know. His first wife. His first child's mother. If it was up to him, especially if he had known about Kristian, he would've married

149

Austynn." I stared out the window and watched the waves crash against the cliff. The central air blasted through the vents. Jerome brushed against me, as he wrapped a blanket around me, giving me chills.

"How did you know I was cold?" I asked as I watched the waves recede into the lake before I settled in a corner of Jerome's brown leather sectional.

"Goosebumps," Jerome said as grazed my forearm with his fingertip.

"You're observant," I said.

"I try to be," Jerome said. There was something about Jerome; something about the way he watched me.

"How are you holding up? Like on a scale from 1-10...how bad do you want to kill your best friend right now?" He asked as he handed me a glass filled midway with Ciroc on the rocks.

"I'm hovering somewhere in the high thirties," I said softly as I swirled the drink around in the glass. "And she is not my friend. Obviously. Ashley has and always will be more of a friend to Chris than to me. Do you know she said, 'you can't be that mad at me. It wasn't my secret to tell.' Yet she was able to blurt it out so easily in front of everyone? Ashley is just as crazy as Chris. And I'm am too through with her."

"To her defense, she was inebriated. She may not have intended to tell you at all."

"Agreed. And that's what makes it so bad. She only told me because she was drunk and upset at something else. And none of that excuses destroying a 20-year friendship and a marriage."

"No...It doesn't," he conceded.

"I always knew I would end up getting hurt. It's like I should've known better but since I knew who Chris was from the beginning...I didn't think I had to worry. Maybe Chris was just a mistake from the beginning."

"Do you regret marrying him?"

"I regret a lot of things," I said. I hadn't thought about it until the question came up. I paused to analyze it. "Chris was everything I wanted in a man yet he fell short of what I needed in a husband."

"How so?"

"Chris and I get along really well. Our friendship masks our relationship flaws. But there's no romanticism to our dynamic. It's as though I have always suspected I wasn't the woman he was in love with. I never knew for sure because Chris never showed me anything but a great partnership. There was just something that I couldn't figure out with him...I just brushed it off. I didn't realize it was that he was secretly in love with someone else. I thought I could love him back to life.

"It's crazy. It was always her. And my ass was just as stuck on stupid. I loved him to the death of me. Why couldn't he love me back?"

Jerome comforted me with a rub on the back. We sat in silence as the wind whistled outside the window. I looked at my phone's screen flashing Chris's cell phone number.

"I should go," I said as I ignored his call for the ninth time since I left the house.

"It's too late to go back," he said.

"I think I'll just go home now," I said as I began to gather my things. I stood up and instantly felt dizzy. I shook it off and walked toward the door. I swayed and staggered into the kitchen. "The floor must be unleveled," I said aloud before I leaned against the island.

"You can't leave in the state your in," Jerome pleaded. "I'd feel so bad if anything happened to you. Just camp out here. I have plenty of room." Jerome sensed my skepticism.

"At least until the rain stops," he added. Lightning flashed across the sky and the rumble of thunder followed seconds later. A news broadcast interrupted a basketball game that played on TV.

"Please remain indoors," the broadcast anchor said. Before any details, the power cut off. As sirens went off in the distance, Jerome ignited the fireplace to illuminate the room and keep us warm as the liquor began to wear off. We sat shoulder-to-shoulder underneath a quilted throw. As sparks flickered behind the screen, we laughed at work shenanigans and office gossip.

Jerome got up to refresh our drinks. He returned to the den with a glass half-full of Crowne Royal and a water bottle.

"Guess which one is yours," he said as he shook the bottle of water.

"I'll take the glass," I replied. Jerome chuckled then obliged by handing me the glass. "I don't usually drink brown liquor. I'm a Ciroc girl, as you know. The brown always pushes my former hood chick personality to the forefront," I said as I lifted my glass with a smile. I took a sip then raised the glass again. "To the brown." Jerome chuckled. He put his head down then looked back at me, gazing.

"What is it? Why are you staring at me?"

"It's just…" Jerome was hesitant. He leaned forward. The smell of his cologne sent a chill down my spine. "I love the way you dress."

"Are you flirting with me?" I asked. Jerome shrugged as a sly grin tugged at the corners of his lips.

"It depends…is it working?"

"No. Because that compliment won't work," I said.

"Why not?"

"Of course you love how I dress," I said after taking a gulp of my drink. I stood up and twirled around. "I always serve looks. honey. Designer from head to toe."

"You dress fly. That's a fact," Jerome complimented.

"I know," I boasted. "So try again."

"You have a beautiful smile," Jerome shot. "You should show it more."

"Well, thank you for bringing it out of me," I sighed and sipped. "With all of this Austynn mess...I just...I'm really blown away by it. It's a nice change to have someone see me for me, instead of try to change me, you know? I'm glad we met. It's like you don't see me as a backup or a second choice." I could tell the drinks I've had since I left my house were getting to me. I started to ramble on about the nothings of life.

"Can I kiss you?" Jerome asked sweetly, like an innocent child.

"What?" I heard him, I was just taken aback by his direct request. Jerome grabbed the drink from my hand and placed it on the side table.

"Can I kiss you?" He repeated. He leaned forward. I inched back.

"Can I get a pillow?" I asked, suddenly feeling like I need to produce space between us.

"I can be your pillow," Jerome said as he leaned back into the couch cushions. He motioned for me to come closer.

"No," I said slowly. "Can I have my drink back?"

"Only if you agree to stay here," he said.

"I can't do that. I needed to cool off. Maybe coming here wasn't the best idea," I realized.

"Please don't leave me," Jerome pleaded, which immediately creeped me out.

"Leave you? I'm flattered you think of me like that," I said. "But I didn't come here for any of this. I thought we were friends."

"We are friends. We are. But you can't deny this," Jerome said and pointed to me and him. "I really want you, and only you," Jerome said as he licked his lips.

"Can't you tell? I compliment you on a regular. I even entertained your silly idea to link up with your girl. I'm doing all of this because...you're the most beautiful woman I've ever seen. The way you make me feel when I'm with you."

"I should go," I said as I arose off of the couch. "Your attempt to make me feel better is actually freaking me out a bit."

"My apologies," Jerome said softly. He grabbed my hand and gently tugged me back to the couch. "I kind of like you and the liquor got me coming on a little stronger than I would normally."

"A little? Try a lot, sir," I said.

"My bad. Forgive me if I made you feel uncomfortable."

"Just a little," I admitted.

"You can't really blame me. You showed up at my door, late night and drunk, mad at your man. All the signs were there. It's a shame. I must have misunderstood the signals...I couldn't have imagined it. But I apologize if I misread them. Listen, camp out here. Do what you need to do to sober up. I'd feel bad if anything happened to you," Jerome said. "The storm should be over soon. I'll go get you that pillow then I'll lock myself upstairs in the bedroom. Deal?"

"Deal," I said somberly. Jerome's footsteps grew faint as he made his way up the stairs. I stumbled out of the half-bath after dousing my face with faucet water. I hoped it would sober me up faster so I could drive home sooner but all it did was sting my eyes. Jerome had left two King sized pillows on the couch next to the throw blanket.

"I didn't even hear him come back downstairs," I said out loud but to myself. I grabbed one of the pillows to snuggle up with on the large sectional. I checked the time. It was nearly five a.m. I set my cell phone alarm to ring at 6 a.m. "A power nap should hurry this soberness along," I reasoned. I dozed off.

I woke up unable to breathe. There was a crushing heaviness on my chest. I momentarily struggled to figure out where I was; still a bit disoriented from mixing dark and clear liquor earlier. I inhaled a deep breath and looked around. The room was pitch black. There was a glimmer of light peeking through the blinds of the only window in the room. I was no longer on the couch in the living room. I was lower, closer to the floor. I tried to get up again.

"Oh you like it rough," Jerome whispered as he kissed my neck and moaned. I tried to get up again, somehow unable to lift my arms. It was as if I was attempting to lift a 150-pound bench press.

"Don't fight it," Jerome said with a whisper in my ear. He forcefully held my wrists together above my head.

"Please stop," I asked. His strength overpowered my might. He began dry humping me before releasing one of my hands. I began to panic as he reached into his sweatpants. As I tried to maneuver out of his distracted grasp Jerome rammed his knee into my thigh. I frantically patted myself down to check for my clothes. My shirt was pulled up exposing half of my bra. Jerome forcefully grabbed my breast in his free hand.

"Where are my pants?" I asked as I patted the bare skin of my thighs. At my ankles. I struggled to get free as I felt a hard poke on my inner thigh, then a thrust from his pelvis. Each touch made me cringe. The more I fought the heavier he became.

"Get off of me," I said.

"I'm sorry," Jerome said as he jerked off to complete his attack. I awkwardly put my clothes back on. As Jerome lay on a nearly deflated air mattress. I went into the bathroom. I looked in the mirror. Fighting back tears with sniffles. I splashed water on my face. I left the faucet running as I tried to compose my emotions.

"This has been a hell of a day," I said. I went back into the room to find my cell phone. As I searched high and low for it, Jerome began to doze off. I found it in a crevice between the mattress and the wall. Half-dressed, I gathered up all of my belongings, held them close and snuck out as quietly and as quickly as I could.

Chris
Heaven Sent
"When love won't let you walk away and you can't help who you love..." - Keyshia Cole

I stared at the ceiling as the darkness of the night dawned into a new day. I didn't sleep through the night. I couldn't. I tossed and turned uneasy that Taylor wasn't home yet. I checked my cell phone for the hundredth time. I rubbed the back of my neck and sighed. It was reaching eight o'clock in the morning and I still hadn't received any contact from Taylor.

Throughout the night, she ignored all of my calls. No texts. No returned calls. Not even a smoke signal. Taylor has never been this upset. I reached for my phone and scrolled through Taylor's social media for a clue as to where she could be - or at least piece together her night. Taylor only posted her Gucci bags, luxury lunches and catwalk-ready selfies, showing off her #outfitoftheday.

After 45 minutes of wasted time, scrolling through pictures, status updates and memes, I got out of bed and ran the shower water. I perfected the cool/hot ratio and let it run over my back for a while. I couldn't shake the uneasiness I'd been feeling. I put on comfortable clothes and grabbed the orange juice out of the fridge. I debated with myself on calling Ashley. If anyone had an update for me, it would be Taylor's best friend.

"Thanks for keeping your promise by the way," I said when she finally answered my call. "You nearly ruined my marriage with your tipsy tongue."

"Wait, what? Hello to you, too," Ashley said as she yawned three times.

"Have you heard from Taylor? She didn't come home last night," I said.

"I haven't seen Taylor since last night. She's upset with me, all thanks to you," Ashley said. "And she hasn't answered any of my calls."

156

"I swear I didn't think she'd take it this bad. In the four years that we've been married, she has never slept one night away from me."

"Could you say the same?" Ashley retorted.

"What are you insinuating?"

"I heard about your late Thursday nights at work," Ashley said. "And we both know how much you love you some Austynn, I mean work."

"Whatever. Austynn works an evening shift every other Thursday. I watch Kristian while she's at work. I couldn't tell Taylor about that without confessing to everything so I told her I was at work, which wasn't a lie."

"Why not? You're supposed to tell your wife everything and not keep stuff - the important stuff- from her. Especially if you know how she reacts."

"She hates to share me with my responsibilities," I admitted.

"Taylor is crazy about you, literally and figuratively. She would've found out in a matter of time. She's more investigative than Black Twitter. That's the whole reason why you didn't want me to tell her," Ashley reminded me. "And when it slipped...I honestly didn't think that you hadn't told her yet. It was an honest mistake, on my part. You hid it for your own reasons."

"It's not even on you, Ashley Jay," I admitted. "I'm mature enough to know I messed up by keeping this from her. Taylor is supposed to be my rider. She *has* to forgive me, right?"

"That's the problem with men. Always want a woman to forgive them instead of not doing a behavior that needs to be forgiven."

"That's unrealistic, Ashley. Nobody is perfect. And love and forgiveness go hand in hand."

"Why does loving you have to include forgiving you for something that you wouldn't forgive her for? It's all so..." Ashley paused in frustration. "When are you going to be mature enough to know that everyone has

157

a breaking point? At what point do men realize there are consequences to the choices you make?"

"Just give me a call if you hear from Taylor," I said.

"Chris, let me be perfectly clear, this is not my fault. You should've told Taylor a long time ago."

"Maybe, but you definitely didn't help the situation," I reminded. "Just keep me posted if you hear from her, please."

"You do the same," Ashley said. I glanced at my phone to check the time. Noon. It's been a little over 12 hours since I've last seen Taylor but I couldn't file a police report for another 12 hours. And when I do what will I say? My wife left in the middle of the night after learning I fathered a child with my ex and I kept it from her for months, told her best friend not to tell her....they won't believe she's missing. They will think she left me. And rightfully so. My cell phone rang. I jumped to answer it, and the device nearly fumbled out of my hand.

"Hi, Dad," Kristian said on the other end of the call. "Dad sounds weird," he said with a laugh.

 "Hi, little Kris," I said. "How's your day going?"

"Pretty good," he said. "I need a ride. Daddy Keith didn't bring Mommy's car back," Kristian disclosed. "Can you take me to karate practice? It's at three."

"Where's your mom?" I asked Kristian. Seconds later I heard him hand the phone to her.

"What's up Austynn," I said. I also checked the pile of old mail in the entryway drawer. I shuffled through some papers in Taylor's briefcase before finding her work laptop.

"Uh oh. What's wrong?" I loved how Austynn could tell something bothered me by my tone.

"Taylor is kind of...missing," I said. "And it's all because of you."

"Come again?" Austynn was confused.

"You're the reason for all of this. You came out of nowhere with this news about Kristian being mine and now Taylor is missing because I couldn't tell her fast enough."

"Ok. Calm down, first. How do you know she's missing?"

"She left late last night. It had to be after one o'clock in the morning. And I haven't been able to reach her since. And it's all because you had to tell me about Kristian."

"You needed to know and she needs to understand that it's not about her. Taylor knew how close we were. She may feel threatened that her fairytale isn't real."

"Everyone knew how close we were but I moved on from you when I had Kaila. I have been committed to Taylor. I've been committed to this marriage since I've been in it."

"I mean, it is what it is," Austynn said.

"I just don't understand how you can be so nonchalant about this."

"Marriage isn't for everyone, Chris. And sometimes the fairytale is accepting an ugly circumstance. Marriage requires putting in the work to make it actually work, which is why most marriages end," Austynn said as if she was speaking from her own experience. "No one wants to be accountable for their own demons but want to point out someone else's."

"This is your fault, Austynn. You weren't honest - with any of us. Not Keith or me. Now my wife is missing. She's gone, Austynn."

"Again, calm down. You're overreacting. It could just be the timing of it all. Taylor may just need time to process everything."

"I'll be there at two to pick Kristian up," I said. As soon as I hung up the call with Austynn my phone rang. I jumped. It was Mr. Jax. I was a bit reluctant to answer, fearing a lecture I wasn't in the mood for; especially considering I had no idea where Taylor was and even less of a clue on how to explain why she left.

"Hi Chris," he said cheerfully. "I need you to pick up Kaila."

"Ok. That's no problem. How is she now? How'd she do on the plane?"

"Kaila has been asking for her mom since she got off the plane. She was up the entire time. A full 13-hour flight and a layover in Detroit. She hadn't fell asleep yet. She's been whining for Taylor the whole time."

"Did you call Taylor?"

"I did. She didn't answer when I reached out today. I spoke to her last night before our flight took off. She was pretty upset. She cried; said she needed to disappear to cool down because you two weren't seeing eye-to-eye. I assumed she went out of town to the lakehouse, like she always does when she needs to get away."

"So she's at the lakehouse? It's wasn't that bad."

"Well, you do know that her mother suffered from depression, right? And everyone knows about Eric's mental illness. Taylor has learned to identify what triggers her and she copes in her own way."

"How much did she tell you about last night?" I said, wondering how much of our personal business Taylor disclosed to Mr. Jax.

"Relax. Taylor isn't the type to tell me all her business. Taylor wouldn't want me to overreact if it's not necessary but she mentioned you lack proper communication skills to be in a healthy marriage. She didn't give me all the details," Mr. Jax noted. "But I can read between the lines."

"That's it, huh?" I asked my father-in-law, feeling like that minute information was too much.

"I'm sure Taylor has a lot of attitude to deal with. I know her wisecracks and snappy wit can annoy anyone but she's a gem. She's loyal to a fault and she loves you."

"I love her, too. I just wish she would be a little more flexible and less rigid with what she thinks our relationship should look like. Everyone's relationship is not supposed to look the same...the same principles of love should apply. Taylor needs to comprehend that."

"Don't act innocent," Mr. Jax commanded. "Trust is easily broken and it's harder to rebuild it than it is to maintain it."

"I understand. I think I hear what you're saying. I just want Taylor to come home. If you talk to her, make sure you tell her that, please."

"I will," Mr. Jax replied.

"What time do you want me to pick up Kaila? I planned on going in to work."

"No worries, Chris. Kaila can stay until you're off. What time are you going in?"

"I really miss my munchkin so I will pick her up as soon as I get off," I said.

"See you soon," Mr. Jax said. I left the house at 2:30 in the afternoon to pick Kristian up.

As I drove through the streets of East Providence, I checked every alley, backroad and hidden route for Taylor. Every stop light, I gripped the steering wheel and glanced in both directions to see if I spotted any sign of Taylor or her truck before the light changed.

I pulled up to Kristian's door at 2:45 and honked the horn. Kristian darted outside of the apartment building as Austynn stood in the doorway. She waved. I waved back.

"You can pick him up too, right? He'll be done in an hour and a half," she said without allowing me to answer.

"I still have to pick up Kaila across town," I said. "And I have to stop by the station to cash in a favor.

"And...you don't think you can do all of that in ninety minutes?" Austynn asked with a slight attitude.

"Where's your car?"

"Keith took it," she said.

161

"I didn't realize you were still in contact with him."

"He's going through a lot," she said. "He did just find out the son he raised isn't his son."

"Because of you!" I said. "When are you going to realize this is all because of you and your lies?"

"Lies? Chris, I understand you're upset since you don't know where your wife is, but you don't have to lash out."

"It's the truth Austynn. I finally see it now. You've been using this tragedy to your advantage with him and now with me."

"I really thought Keith was Kristian's father." she said.

"No," I said. "You *wanted* him to be. You wanted to be with Keith so bad that you wished our son was his. You caused this."

"Keith and I were already together," Austynn said. "I wasn't supposed to be dealing with you."

"Ok. Let's leave that right there," I said before I got into my feelings about her latest sentiment. "I'll be back in a hour. We can talk more about this later."

As I waited for Kristian's karate lesson to end, I stopped by the precinct where a friend of mine worked. I walked into the lobby of the station and signed my name on a visitor's list attached to a clipboard on the counter. The police officer behind the glass pulled the clipboard through a small slit.

"What's the name?" he asked.

"The name?" I repeated.

"Of who you're bailing out. What's her..or his name?" the officer asked.

"I'm here to see Officer Brown," I said, confused.

"Oh. Have a seat. Give me one minute to find him" the officer said in a more cheerful tone. I waited on a wooden bench for ten minutes before my old friend emerged from behind the padlocked door.

"Chris, it's been a while. How have you been," he said as he extended his arm to give me a handshake. I pulled him into a hug.

"I need a favor, Rick," I whispered.

"Anything," he said as he pulled away. He sensed the seriousness in my tone.

"I need to file a police report." His eyebrow raised but he remained silent as I continued. "For a stolen car." I gave him the make and model of Taylor's truck. He jotted it down on a pocket-sized notebook.

"When was the last time you've seen it?"

"On Bassett Street. Around 12 a.m."

"Are you the owner?"

"It's my wife's car," I admitted.

"And where is she?"

"She's out of town. At her family's lakehouse." Rick raised his eyebrow again.

"When did she leave?"

"Friday night," I said. "She left from work. She went to happy hour with her friends and left the car there parked. She took Lyft and when I went to pick her car up, it was gone."

"Why didn't you report it sooner?"

"I thought my wife may have change her mind and drove. I spoke with her father, Mr. Jaxon, and confirmed."

"Mr. Jaxon Smith?"

"Thee one and only," I said.

"I'll have my team escalate this one," Rick said.

"Ok, thank you," I said as we shook hands. "I appreciate you."

Rick ripped the paper out of his notepad and handed it to the officer behind the glass.

"Make this a stat," he said as she typed the information into her workstation. She scribbled a few numbers on a scrap paper and handed it to Officer Brown.
It was the case number and the officer assigned to the case. I thanked both officers before I left out the precinct to get Kristian. Kristian stood with his sensei outside of the building. Kristian was the last kid left.

"Am I late?" I asked. "It's my first time."

"No worries," the woman said as she guided Kristian to the backseat of my car. "We welcome change." She smiled. Kristian buckled his seatbelt and waved as we drove off.

I dropped Kristian off with a large cheese pizza, a bagful of some of his favorite snacks, Oreos, Pop-tarts and Cheetos and a few school supplies. I also put a fifty dollar bill in his jean pocket.

"Make sure you have your mom check your pockets okay? Kristian nodded before he jumped out the car, sporting the biggest smile. He was determined to carry all three of his bags and the pizza without assistance."

"I got it, Dad."

"Ok. Have a good night," I said. "I'll bring you by Mama's house next weekend. Listen to your mom and mind your manners, young man."

"Yes, sir," he said. I honked the horn and waved as Kristian wobbled and swayed inside. As I started to drive away, Austynn ran out the building in a gray satin robe. She tapped on the trunk of the car to get my attention before I was fully in the street.

"Thank you for doing this. It's a big help," Austynn said then paused. "I may need your assistance with Kristian again tomorrow. Will you be able to pick him up? I haven't heard back from Keith about the car." I checked my wristwatch and avoided eye contact.

"In case you haven't noticed, my wife is still missing. And I still have to go pick up Kaila."

"Ok."

"We are going to have to set some ground rules, going forward."

"Rules?"

"Yes. rules and a schedule,"

"A schedule? For what exactly?"

"For structure," I said. "This has to make sense for both of us and I can't keep being at your beckon call because you have my child."

"Whoa. Ok. I see Taylor has gotten to you. You would never have said this before. Ok. We can talk. Will child support be included in that conversation?"

"If it needs to be," I said. I chuckled. Taylor was right. This chick felt like she hit the lotto. Baby mothers always want you to finance their lifestyle just because they have your child.

"Even with me giving cash, regularly, you want to discuss child support?

"It's only right for Kristian to live like your other child," Austynn admitted.

"And what will you bring to the equation? You know what? Don't even answer that. I'll have my attorney draft a parenting agreement and financial plan. You can have your lawyer review the documents," I said in a formal tone.

"Ok," she said as I sped off. I smirked. Austynn didn't know this side of me...I just met him myself.

My Mercedes wrapped around the curves of the Blackstone's circular driveway as smooth as butter slides down a warm biscuit. I left the car running and rang the bell. Mr. Jax answered with Kaila, half-sleep in his arms. He motioned to his butler, who carried Kaila's luggage to the car and loaded it in the trunk like a hotel concierge.

"Quick shift?" he asked as he handed Kaila over to my open arms. He kissed her forehead.

"I just had to finish up some paperwork. Have you gotten in touch with Taylor yet?"

"No. I think it's best to give her some space," Mr. Jax said. "One thing I know about Taylor is that she hates for any situation to be forced on her. Give her time. She'll call when she's ready."

"I'm just getting a little worried about her," I revealed.

"I understand," he said with a pat on the shoulder. "Give her some space. She'll come around."

"Get some rest, Pops," I said. "Thank you for everything."

"Don't mention it," Mr. Jax said before disappearing into his mansion. I stopped by my mother's house. Mama Matthews missed Kaila and demanded I bring her by the moment she landed.

After a brief visit with grandma, I hoped Kaila would tire herself out and go to sleep on the ride home. She did not. Instead, she whined and wailed the whole time.

"Mommy isn't home," I said. I had to deal with the aftermath of my decisions. I couldn't accept the narrative that Taylor left me. That was a hard pill to swallow. *I know she loves me. I know it. This Kristian thing wouldn't send her packing...so where is she?*

I parked into the garage, gathered Kaila's things and went into the house to prepare dinner. I reheated the plate of baked ziti my mom packed for us.
I played princess tea time with Kaila after dinner and then got her ready for bed.

Bath time turned chaotic because I wasn't Taylor. Kaila hated how I rushed her through bathtime, while Taylor allowed Kaila to swim in her dirty bathwater until her fingertips wrinkled. Post bathtime, Taylor would wash Kaila's hair, which hung past her shoulders, then twist it up while Kaila played on her tablet.

"Where's Mommy," Kaila asked. "I want my mommy!" she wailed as I attempted to brush her hair into a ponytail. I groaned along with her. I wanted Taylor to come back just as much as Kaila did.

"Baby, I know you want Mommy, but she isn't here," I said. "I hope she comes back soon, too." I attempted to be more Taylor like and find my patience as Kaila threw herself to the floor, convulsing and screaming for her mother. I tried to calm Kaila down but nothing worked.

After two runs of Princess and the Frog, a reading of two Dr. Seuss books cover to cover and a bribe of candy and ice cream for breakfast, Kaila finally stopped crying and began to drift off to sleep. I cuddled close to Kaila under her Princess Tiana blanket and dozed off. I was startled out of my sleep by the doorbell. I quickly shuffled to the door. I peeked out the side panel window.

My heart sank when I spotted a police car parked on the street. Another ring of the bell made my heart sink deeper. I took a deep breath. My heart raced and my palms clammy. I took a deep breath again before I opened the door slowly.

Two uniformed police officers stood on the other side. I could feel the creases form on my forehead as my eyes narrowed.

"Mister Matthews," one of them said before glancing at his partner.

"Yes," I said. I stuck my nose in the air. My heart palpitated. "I assume you're here because you've located my wife - I mean - my wife's car."

"Yes, we did. That's what we are here to discuss. May we come in?"

Ray
Say Goodbye
"There's never a right time..." - Chris Brown

I stood outside of the main building of RI Hospital near Zecchino Pavilion. I spotted Ashley as she dispersed from a crowd of nurses as she took her lunch break. I lurked behind her as she walked toward Dudley Street Cafe, her spot for a quick lunch between shifts.

As Ashley ordered her usual: turkey club on wheat with no mayo, lite mustard with lettuce, no tomatoes and extra pickles, I snuck up behind her. I pulled a $20 bill out of my wallet and handed it to the cashier.

"Add a bottle of Dasani water and that overpriced energy drink. Not that one," I said as he reached for a small ten ounce silver and blue can. "The black one; yes, the Rockstar." I put the change in my pocket and guided Ashley to a small table in the back. I pulled her chair out for her and sat down in the seat across from her.

"What are you doing here?" Ashley asked.

"I thought it would be a pleasant surprise," I said. "I'm glad to see you're still wearing my ring. That means we're still on."

"That means we are waiting for that DNA test before we move forward."

"Well, you know, that's why I'm here."

"The DNA test?"

"I have to meet Alana for a doctor's appointment," I said.

"You just jumped right in, huh? I'm sure she's happy about that."

"She is. She always loved her some me." I chuckled. "They all do."
Ashley nodded as she munched on her potato chips. She took two

169

bites, which finished off half of her sandwich. She offered me the other half. I declined. She shrugged and took a sip of her water.

"You know...she's due next month. And our wedding is four months away?"

"So you still think we're going through with the wedding," she asked. I nodded.

"We have to. You're not working all that overtime for no reason."

"Yes," she said with a chuckle. The laugh was to lighten the seriousness of her tone, but I knew exactly she meant.

"Depending on those results," I said. Ashley wouldn't go through with the wedding if I was the father of Alana's child. And I knew why. "Are you still coming to the graduation?" I asked.

"I wouldn't miss it," Ashley said. "I may just drop off a gift to them. I don't want to run into your maybe baby mother. How's Shirley?"

"Shirley is actually doing well after checking herself into rehab. She'll be there for another month or so. She has to do the full 90 days this time. She's been sober for 39 days, now. She wants to be around for the wedding. She knows she'll miss the twins' graduation and she doesn't want to miss out on anything else."

"That's good to hear," Ashley said. "I'm glad she's making progress. Prayer works."

"I swear, I'm lucky to have met you," I gushed. "You're always positive."

"Positivity is a must in this negative world we live in," Ashley said.

"We're still together, you know," I said to Ashley with a slight grin. She rolled her eyes to the ceiling and got up from the chair.

"What's that?" She asked with a matched grin. "I don't know about all of that."

"Don't be like that Ashley," I said. "You heard what I said. I mean it. Keep wearing that ring, girl. You're taken. Forever status."

"It was good to see you," she said with a smile as she gave me a church hug. I pulled her into a bear hug. "Give me a call later. We'll talk more about it then."

I walked Ashley back into the hospital building. We hugged again before Ashley trotted back into the emergency entrance. I checked the time as I waited for Alana to show up for her appointment. When I noticed her car parked in the valet loop, I walked to the information center in the lobby.

"What floor do you get an ultrasound for pregnancy on," I asked the lady behind the counter.

"You need the women's center on the fourth floor," she said. "Take those elevators to the right to the left wing then cross the pavilion."

"Thank you, beautiful," I flirted. I followed her directions and got off the elevator. I looked around for a clue of where to go next. An elderly woman walked through a door with a slew of people in the waiting room. I followed behind her.

Alana spotted me as soon as I hit the door of the waiting area. She waved me down and patted the empty seat next to her.

"I already checked in," she said without looking up from the pages of a parenting magazine she flipped through.

"How long do these things usually last," I asked, looking around the room. "Will we be able to find out today?" I whispered.

"I don't think so. I'm too far along for the amniocentesis and you can't afford the CVS test."

"Why wouldn't I be able to afford a test from CVS?"

"No. It's a chroionic villus sampling test. It's $1600."

"You're right about that. How much is the other test?"

171

"It's $350."

"We're just have to wait until the baby is born," I said. She smiled then buried her head back into the magazine.

"Just six weeks left," she said. I began to fidget around the small chair. The longer it took, the more antsy I became. Name after name had been called except Alana's. We sat through two hour-long talk shows before they called Alana's name.

We were ushered into the back clinic by a BBW with the roundest ass I've ever seen. Her waist was tiny. Her tight scrubs hugged her curves like a newborn nursing on his mother's bosom. I smiled as we followed behind her. Alana hit my arm.

"You're damn near drooling," she said. I shrugged. I couldn't help it. Before we were put into an exam room, the nurse charted Alana's weight, blood pressure and heart rate. She handed her a folded hospital gown and asked Alana to change. "You're in room 3," she said pointing.

Once in the exam room, Alana changed. She emerged from the bathroom and climbed onto the papered exam table. Alana placed the heels of her feet into stirrups. Alana's doctor softly knocked on the door before he opened it. Her doctor was a young, white guy in his late 30s, with reddish blonde hair, blue eyes and a full beard - Ed Sheeran vibes.

"I'm Doctor Jefferson," he said as he shook my hand. He then waved politely to Alana before walking over her. He leaned over and placed his hand on her shoulder.

"How are you? How's the little one?" He asked before he walked to the sink to wash his hands. He washed his hands as he recited the ABCs. He then repeated the process, singing the alphabet song backwards. He pulled down three paper towels, patted his palms then tossed the damp crumbled pieces into a step-on receptacle. He plucked a pair of plastic gloves from a box on the counter, sat down in a chair on wheels and swiveled around in between Alana's spread legs.

"Being this is your first pregnancy, first borns are stubborn and known for staying in a little longer," the doctor said as he rolled down what resembled an extra long sheath onto a skinny probe then inserted it inside. Alana squirmed, showing her discomfort.

"Relax," I said, "You've had bigger." Dr. Jefferson chuckled, which he immediately covered up with a cough.

"Since you've been experiencing some spotting, let's take a look," he said as he moved the probe around. A blurry image popped on the mounted monitor. "It looks like the baby is putting some pressure on your cervix," he said, pointing to the screen. "That may be the cause for the bleeding. She's putting on a show." I squinted to make out the blobs I saw on screen as "the baby," as the doctor traced and circled the same areas with his finger.

"That's her heart," he said as Alana cheesed, gazing at the flickering on the monitor.

"You've got eight weeks left," Dr. Jefferson said as he tapped the keyboard paused then clicked the mouse a few times before a series of sonograms spewed from a small printer. He handed me the photos. I passed them to Alana without looking at the snapshots.

"Eight weeks puts your due date well into October," I realized aloud.

"You know my cycle is irregular," Alana replied with a slight shrug of the shoulders. "And it doesn't matter. We were getting it in *well* into your little engagement...so I'm not worried," Alana said as I peeked where the doctor poked. I smirked and suddenly remembered why Alana and I dealt with each other. But the dirty images dissipated as soon as Alana opened her mouth.

"Have you thought of baby names for our baby girl yet?" Alana asked.

"I hadn't really thought about it, to be honest," I said with a shrug.

"Raina Davis King," Alana said proudly.

"Like Raina as in Ghost's daughter?" I asked.

"Or like our names, Ray and Alana put together."

"Our names put together is more like Raylana, Lana Rae, Larae or Rayla. Not Raina."

"I like Raina so it's Raina."

"It's your baby," I said.

"Everything looks good," Dr. Jefferson said as he slid away from between Alana's legs. "Your blood pressure is a bit low. We're going to monitor it so you need to come back - every week until your due date. Get dressed." He patted her exposed thigh. "And we'll schedule your appointment for next week." The doctor excused himself as he pulled the curtain back and left the room.

"You hear that, Ray? Every week. I expect you to be there," Alana said as she got dressed. I bit my lip as she bent over to pull her legs into her jeans. I rubbed her butt and she swatted my hand away.

"I thought you wanted that," I said. Alana rolled her eyes. I held the door open for her. She didn't look pregnant from behind. We stood behind a couple in line as we waited at checkout. The man rubbed the woman's shoulders and whispered in her ear.

"You gotta do better," Alana said as I stood beside her as she watched the couple in front of her. "Like him."

"You need to say goodbye to whatever you had in mind," I said to her. "I'm already taken. Even if that baby is mine, we can't be anything more than cool."

"If the baby is yours? Stop insulting me like that, King."

"It's just a reminder. I'm only here because we're cool and there's a slight possibility the kid is mine. Miniscule, minute window of a chance I could be your baby daddy. However, I am not interested in anything more than that. Finding out who's the daddy is my only concern."

Alana ignored me as we made our way to the front of the line. After nearly ten minutes of small talk and catching with the lady behind the desk, she confirmed Alana's next appointment. Alana put the reminder card into her purse and wobbled out of the lobby.

"I'm not sharing you with her!" Alana said as we left the doctor's office. We waited for the elevator in thought-provoking silence. "How does Ashley feel about all of this?" she pried as she waddled to valet, who retrieved her car quickly. "I know you need a ride," she said as she patted the passenger seat of her Mustang. "We both know Ashley isn't built for all of this. Do you think she's ready for stepmommy duties?"

"And why is that any concern of yours? Let that be my problem. I swear you don't know how to worry about yourself. Ashley and I are fine. Our bond is unbreakable, baby." Alana rolled her eyes, dismissively.

"We'll see," she said.

"It sounds like you're plotting. Don't try anything stupid. I swear it will be you that will end up disappointed."

"Get over yourself already. You know I can give you everything she's not giving you - and then some."

"Alana, we've been over this...Ashley satisfies me in ways that are beyond anything physical you can ever offer."

"Sexual," Alana corrected. "I can offer you any and everything sexually that your lil' fiance won't do - and you know it. Just the thought of my face buried in your sheets, ass up in the air, and my wet cat soaking your big Daddy dick," Alana said as a seductive grin developed. "Look at Prince, jumping for some attention now. I know what he likes," she hissed as she grazed her fingertips across my lap. Prince pitched a tent in my gray sweats.

"Those pregnancy hormones must have gotten to your head because you're definitely talking out of your neck."

"Remember who I am," Alana demanded.

"And who's that?" I asked, amused at Alana's audacity.

"The same one you always come to when your girl of the moment can't get you right," Alana said with confidence.

"That's who you used to be," I corrected. "Now...you're just some crazy girl who won't let go of the past."

"Well," Alana said with a long pause. "I will gladly take on the role of mother of your future child," Alana said.

"You'd take any role, let's be honest," I said.

"So is everything still on track with the wedding? Ashley is really going to stay with you during this whole baby situation?"

"Me and Ashley are good. You can stop asking. And even if it wasn't, I wouldn't tell you."

"That's rude, King."

"No, it's not. It's none of your business."

"I can't with you. You are really feeling this girl."

"We've been over this...Ashley ain't going nowhere...not if I can help it...damn."

"Well...neither am I," Alana said. "And that's something you'll have to get used to and she is going to have to accept that I am going to be a permanent part of your life, period. End of story."

"When will you accept that Ashley will be my wife?"

"Never," Alana said slowly. She laughed.

"Stop being extra. You're going to have to get it at some point, Alana. Even if it wasn't Ashley - it wouldn't be you. I'm sorry." I shrugged.

"Whatever you say King," Alana said as she parked in the rear driveway of my house. "Your newfound love is cute and all but, we both know you. You can't keep your hands off me. I need to pee." Before I had a chance to answer, Alana darted into the house, through the kitchen to the bathroom.

"Hi, Shelley," Alana said to Shelley sat at the kitchen table with a plate full of leftover Chinese takeout in front of her.

"You stay in the kitchen, damn girl," I said as I purveyed her food.

"And you stay with a new chick. Who is that again?" Shelley said as she swatted my hand away.

"That's Alana. She's definitely not new and she's leaving."

"Can I get a glass of apple juice?" Alana asked me when she emerged from the bathroom. "The baby," she said as she patted her bulging belly. I handed her a glass out of the cupboard and searched the fridge.

"We're fresh out of apple juice," I said as I gave her a bottle of orange juice.

"Congratulations," Shelley said to Alana.

"Thanks. Do you want to see pictures?" Alana asked while pulling out the sonogram printouts she received at the doctor's office. "Of your niece." Shelley coughed fried rice out of her mouth and caught it in her hand.

"My niece?" Shelley asked. She looked at me with wide eyes for confirmation. I looked away. Shelley snatched the photos from Alana's hand.

"She looks like Ray already," Alana said.

"How could you tell?" I asked. Alana hovered over Shelley's shoulder pointing at the image.

"I don't see it. Let's not jump to conclusions and wait to see what the tests say."

"The test won't tell you anything I'm not telling you already."

"Ok. Well, let the test talk then. Say less."

"Cool. I'll pick you up for our next appointment."

"I'm going to be at the twins' graduation. I'll make it to the next one."

177

"Or..."Alana said slowly. "I can pick you up from the graduation. The appointment is at four."

"The graduation is over at two and the party starts at four," I said.

"Ashley is taking care of the party," Shelley noted. I glared at her. She shrugged.

"Ok. So that's why you don't want me to come," Alana realized.

"Ok. Time to go. I'll walk you out," I said to her as I ushered her toward the back door.

"But I'm not done with my juice," Alana said as she raised the half-full glass.

"It's fine. Take it with you," I said as I gently pulled her arm. "Let's go." I opened the back door and guided Alana out of the house. As Alana sat down she gulped her juice then shoved the empty glass in my face.

"So...three o'clock next week?"

"No one would be upset if you didn't come to the graduation," I explained.

"You really have to be at the next appointment," she whined. "It's for our baby."

"Man, you're really stressing this whole it's-your-baby thing," I asked with air quotations. "I can get a ride there. I don't need you to swing by, none of that."

"Ok. Thank you," Alana said before adding, "you better be at the appointment or I'm crashing the party. We both know you don't want that."

"Ok. Alana," I said after a deep breath. "You enjoy the rest of your day."

"I'll call you later. You better answer, so you can say good night to your child!"

"Now I know you're crazy," I said.

"Don't say that Ray," Alana said before she sped off. I walked in the house shaking my head. I sat across the table from Shelley who was stingy with the
spoonful of food she had left.

"So what does your fiance, Ashley, say about all of this?" Shelley inquired as she gobbled the last bite. "I can't imagine her accepting all of that drama before she even walks down the aisle."

"Whose side are you on?"

"The right side," Shelley said.

"I wouldn't put it past Alana if all of this is some type of ploy. She has always wanted to be with me. This could all be a game to get me to wife her."

"Why would any sane woman want what you have to offer? Lies on top of betrayal with a sprinkle of deceit. Who wants that?"

"Some women can't resist this pipe game, girl," I said.

"Eww," Shelley said.

"And Alana is crazy, so," I added.

"Well, I don't think she would lie about her child's father." Shelley said.

"Just a second ago you didn't even know who she was...now you're vouching for her?"

"Girl power!"

"More like hoe life!"

"Takes one to know one," Shelley teased. She stuck her tongue out at me and smiled. "But seriously, I don't want you to lose Ashley over this maybe baby."

"You already know Ashley's riding with your boy," I reassured her, even though I questioned it myself.

"You don't sound too sure," Shelley picked up on immediately.

"Ashley loves me. She'll be there for me. Like I would be for her."

"If Ashley was pregnant by one of her exes you would stick around? I wouldn't believe that if Ashley had millions attached to her. It's an ego thing."

"Luckily, that's not my problem. And it's not hers either. That's not my baby. But I'll entertain it."

"You better hope not or you can say goodbye to your future with Ashley."

"I'm really not worried. Ashley knows what's up."

"You are unemployed with a baby on the way. I don't think any woman would sign up for that."

"What do you know?" I asked. I walked out in a huff as I dialed Ashley's number. The phone rang five times before her voicemail came on. I didn't bother to leave a message. She called back two hours later.

"Finally," I said when I answered. "They let you make a call? I was starting to think you were being held hostage."

"I just finished my shift," Ashley said.

"Does that mean you are mine for the rest of the night?"

"I wouldn't say that," she replied.

"What else do you have planned?"

"Recharge and rejuvenation. I have to go back in at 11."

"But you just got off," I said.

180

"I worked seven o'clock in the morning until seven in the evening then I go back in at 11 and I work until seven in the morning." I grunted. "But then I'm off for three days."

"That is a lot of work for someone with a child. Where's Isaiah? Let me guess, his rich grands' house, i mean mansion, excuse me."

"You are in a mood tonight. Does it stem for your doctor's appointment?"

"We have six to eight weeks until the baby is born. And since her blood pressure is high, we have weekly appointments.

"You are throwing me off with all those wes. Are you really invested in this now?"

"I'm simply doing what I think is right. Don't read more into it."

-"And what do you think is right?"

"To be there for my child."

"You don't even know if that's your child yet. What if it isn't? Where is this change of heart coming from all of sudden?"

"It's not a change of heart, just a do-the-right-thing-regardless kind of situation."

"Oh ok. So what else should I know?"

"Next week is the graduation and an appointment. I told her I would be there but she insists that she come and pick me up. She threatened to crash the twins' party if I don't show."

"Is this how she's going to be? Threatening you with her presence at every function? I have a problem with that."

"I do, too. But we're going to be fine. I'm sure of it. Just don't start pulling away now, please."

"You don't think maybe it's for the best?"

"You would really not talk to me until then - even though we are engaged to be married?"

"If it had to - for my own sanity? Yes."

"Who has been in your ear? We are good, Ashley. You don't have anything to worry about. I don't want Alana."

"But she wants you," Ashley said. "And that's dangerous."

"Alana wants everybody. She just loves me."

"Right, and you don't see that as a problem?"

"I see it as what it is. I can't control that girl's feelings. All I know is the feelings aren't mutual. I haven't dealt with that girl since I've been dealing with you. And I could have. So just ride this out with me. Besides, we both know you ain't trying to start over with someone new. You gonna have to tell that whole story again..."

"I will if I have to. We should talk about this another time. When it's necessary. Let's just see what happens with the test," Ashley said quietly.

"Don't get distant, A.J. I need you."

"I know. I'm here for you," Ashley said.

"I swear you are one-of-a-kind. I love you Ashley Jay Johnson."

Chris

Fortunate

"I never felt a feeling so right. I bless the day that I found you." - Maxwell

Ashley emerged from a back room and walked toward me. She stepped lightly on the patterned carpet in her stilettos. Kaila held her hand as she trolleyed behind. The switch of Ashley's hips were heard with every step as the thick of her thighs rubbed against her pantyhose.

"Thank you for taking care of that," I said. "I wouldn't know what to do."

"Miss Amy was too distraught. She had to take a break so I finished her makeup. I did her face so well, Kaila didn't realize and kept nudging her arm until she felt how stiff it was." My mouth released a sound of pain I never heard.

"How are you holding up," Ashley asked me.

"This is hard," I whispered through quivering lips.

"I know," Ashley said as she patted my back. I blew out a deep breath, put my hand to my chest and inhaled. I straightened my posture and held my hand out for Kaila to hold. Two ushers wheeled out a closed casket. One of the clergymen pulled my father-in-law to the podium. I stopped them before they opened the glistening white porcelain casket. I scooped Kaila into my arms and nodded for them to proceed.

"They're ready for you," I said softly. I stared at the angelic face that lay before me. I blew a kiss before she was put display in the main sanctuary.

"Let's take a seat. It's almost time," Ashley said. We walked toward the front pews. People from all over the world made their way to say goodbye to Taylor. Everywhere I turned there was another person offering their condolences and crying harder than some of the family. Faint whispers, small waves of hello and long hugs were the greetings I received as I took a seat. Mama Matthews sat beside me, Kaila on my lap and Mr. Jax, his wife, Miss Amy on the other side.

Isaiah sat with Ashley's parents, Harold and Rita, and Jasmin in the second pew behind us. Poster-sized photos hung high and Taylor's favorite flowers, white lilies, cluttered the altar. A somber, sullen feeling took over as the pews filled. I noticed Austynn walk in with Kristian. They sat in the last pew, close to the exit. I hurried over to her.

Kristian jumped out of his seat and wrapped his arms around my waist. I kneeled down. He had tears in his eyes. I looked at Austynn as I helped Kristian back into his seat.

"You shouldn't be here," I told her.

"It's open to the public," Austynn replied. "And now is a good time from him to meet his little sister." I looked around and caught eye contact with a glaring Ashley. I looked away quickly. I rubbed the nape of my neck. I looked to the ceiling and whispered a silent prayer.

"What's wrong with you?" I asked an unapologetic Austynn. I couldn't see her expression behind her oversized sunglasses and wide brim black fedora. I was sure she could see the disgust on my face. "Now isn't the time for any of this."

"This is nothing. Now go back up there and don't come back here until the service ends. You are the one drawing attention to yourself. We'll talk when it's over," she said as she snuggled close to Kristian and looked over the program. I walked back up to the front row. Ashley stopped me by putting her foot in the aisle. She motioned for me to lean down.

"Is everything ok?" she whispered in my ear. She glanced back at Austynn then back at me.

"Everything is fine," I said. "I've got it under control."

"You better," Ashley said sternly. "Nobody here needs her messing this up for everyone. Not today."

"I got it," I reassured Ashley. I sat down right before the choir sang their first song out of five. The pastor eulogized for nearly an hour. I just sat and gazed at the casket. It was all surreal. It felt like I was everything played out in slow motion - but in real time - like a dubbed martial arts movie. After a half hour of spoken hymns by Rumi, Taylor's favorite writer, what only seemed like two minutes of reflection by Mr. Jax - it was my turn.

I walked to the podium that overlooked the casket as adjusted my cuffs, which exposed the Gucci cufflinks Taylor purchased for one of our anniversaries. I smiled and teared up. I took a deep breath, dabbed the corners of my eyes with a handkerchief then cleared my throat.

"Memories are the worst kind of torture. They sneak up on you and seep into your thoughts. Triggered by a smell, a look, a gift," I said as I adjusted the microphone. "Taylor Smith-Matthews will always be remembered," I said as I adjusted the microphone. "Because everything will always remind me of her. My daughter has her face. My room smells like her favorite perfume. Red Door. It was so fragrant and Taylor only like it because she said it smelled expensive." I managed to laugh. So did the congregation.

"She had so many rules - even with perfume. She used 15 pumps. And Taylor was literal. Five per region: upper body, midsection and don't neglect the lady parts, she'd say. Taylor never sprayed it on her skin because she broke out in hives," I said in a shaky voice. "I never imagined I would have to do my forever without you. You meant the world to me, Taylor. I was fortunate to have you baby. I am so sorry," I said in a cracked voice. I blew a kiss toward the casket as a single tear fell down my cheek. "This is my fault." I broke down and heaved between sobs. "Rest in paradise, my angel."

Mr. Jax comforted me as I approached my seat. Miss Amy dabbed the corners of her eyes with a crumbled tissue she had balled in between her fists. Rita rubbed Miss Amy's back from the second row. Harold held Ashley's mom's hand and hugged Jasmin, who sobbed, uncontrollably. I glanced back and gave Ashley a nod. Ray squeezed and kissed Ashley's hand before she walked toward the podium.

Ashley stood silently for a moment as she scaled the room. I glanced around the room, too. Besides the front two rows, the room was full of people I didn't recognize. It was like a circus full of fake friends and nosy neighbors paying their respects to Taylor hoping to be seen by the other people in attendance. Her social media comments were full of selfies posted with meaningless hashtags that they won't take a second look at after tomorrow.

"Taylor Smith-Matthews was my best friend," Ashley said as she glanced down. "She was my sister from another mister, my voice of reason and my partner in crime. We hung out together, we laughed together and we cried together. Taylor was a bad singer and an even worse cook. But she was always true to who she was. A spoiled daddy's girl who loved her name brands as much as she loved her daughter. Selfish at times and inconsiderate. But she fought for what she believed in and stood by those she loved. She lived to make her daughter smile and she loved her family to the end. She will forever be remembered for her impeccable style and unmatched wit. And she wouldn't have it any other way. I can't imagine life without her presence. But that will be something we all have to deal with," Ashley said as her lips quivered. "Thank you all for coming," she said fighting back tears. "The burial is going to be immediate family only. And will follow the repass, which is taking place now, downstairs. Please join us in the dining area. Just follow the signs."

Ashley walked away from the podium, legs wobbly like Jello, and nearly fell into my arms. We held each other up and wept. My heart was heavier than Taylor's casket.

We walked downstairs together, arms wrapped around each other for support. The family had our food served to us while others waited in a buffet line.

"How could anyone be eating right now?" I wondered as I picked through a loaded plate of food. The chicken was tasteless. The collard greens were too vinegary. The cheese in the lasagna had spoiled...at least that what I got from the smell. The rolls were stale and everything else just looked unappealing. Yet everyone everywhere I looked we stuffing their faces like we aren't about to stuff my better half in a box and dropped into the ground.

"This is now how I'd pictured how we'd spend forever, my angel," I said to Taylor as if she could still hear me. I pulled a chair out to sit down with the family. Isaiah held hands with Kaila as they sat at the family table. Miss Amy rubbed Mr. Jax's back as he buried his face in his hands and sobbed, uncontrollably. Mr. Jax excused himself and retreated to the restroom to compose his emotional outburst.

"She walked into the rain and didn't look back. It was the last time any of us ever saw her again," I overheard Morgan explain before breaking down. I swam in tears. The emotion was suffocating.

I glimpsed around the room for the closest exit. And sprinted toward it as incognito as I could. While I was able to dodge some bystanders and passersby, I literally bumped right into someone.

"Oh my god!" I said as I threw my head back and my hands up, in aggravation. "Excuse me," I said politely as I tried to push my way through the small crowd that formed by the door. "I need some air," I said as I squeezed past it to push through the door of the exit. I noticed Ashley had stepped outside, too. She stood with her back against the wall of the brick building. She had buried her face in her hands and sobbed. She quickly composed herself when she noticed me walking toward her. Ashley put on a phony smile. She wiped her damp cheeks with a wrinkled handkerchief and waved. I looked behind me when I realized she was interacting with someone else.

"Thank you for coming," Ashley mumbled to the man, who looked slightly familiar.

"Ashley Jay, just the person I wanted to run into," the eerily familiar voice said.

"Jerome," she said. He hung his head, just for a moment, then pulled her into an embrace. "I'm surprised you showed up."

"I'm here for you," he said. "It didn't feel right to let you go through this by yourself. How are you holding up? Are you ok," he asked as Ashley. He approached closer. He pulled her into a hug without uttering another word. They held the embrace for just a moment.

"I'm fine," Ashley insisted. She frowned and stepped back. "Chris is the one who's hurting."

"I'm truly sorry for your loss," he said as he extended his hand out to me. I never know how to respond to that because thank you doesn't seem appropriate. I remained silent. "If it makes you feel any better, people

187

die everyday," Jerome said with a shrug. "And everyone has their day," Jerome insisted.

"I understand that people die everyday and everyone dies but she was my best friend. The aunt to my son. She was literally like a sister to me," Ashley said.

"You and her were pretty close too," I said to Jerome, who finally made eye contact.

"That's why I'm here," Jerome said, then turned back to Ashley. "I can't relate to your loss. I haven't experienced anything like this before. But I know you lost your best friend, both of you. I just wanted to pay my respect, because Taylor was cool people," Jerome said. He sounded sincere. "Has anyone heard about the details of that night? Or why she was so upset?" He glared out the side of his eye at me but faced Ashley.

"No," I said. "The police didn't come up with anything. It's only been two weeks since it all happened. The accident. And now this. The police don't really have any leads right now."

"Well, like I said, I'm sorry for your loss," Jerome said. "I'm going to say hello to Mr. Jax before I head out of here. I'm getting transferred to Houston for another project so, I was nice to meet you and again, I'm sorry for your loss," he said before he shook my hand again.

Jerome gave Ashley a hug before he headed inside the building. Ashley and I stayed outside in silence as we watched a slew of mourners disperse from the cathedral. A warm breeze blew as the sun began to set. The family came through the double doors as an all-white Bentley hearse pulled out, slowly from the driveway.

"It's time," Ashley said once she spotted the hearse. "I'm going to head home. Tell Mr. Jax to send Isaiah home later."

"You're not coming to the burial?" I asked.

"I'm going to sit this one out," Ashley said. "Immediate family only. I'm not family, remember?"

"Don't be that way, Ashley."

"You said it. And, now, I'm simply agreeing."

"But Isaiah is going to be there. He needs him mom. And Taylor would've wanted you there."

"I'm not sure if you remember, but Taylor was mad at me, too. That's why she went missing for two days. Because of us. Taylor held a grudge with the preschooler who pulled Kaila's ponytail. She definitely would have taken me off the guest list. I don't blame her, after what I didn't do. Some best friend I am." I could see the guilt behind her tears. I recognized it. I mirrored it.

"Are you sure you're going to be ok to drive?" I asked.

"I'm only headed home," Ashley said. She lingered until everyone got into the limousine, one after the other. She kissed Isaiah goodbye and waved as he stepped into the vehicle.

"I'll pick you up tomorrow morning," Ashley said. "Kaila needs you little man. Mommy will be ok. I have Auntie Morgan to keep me company."

"Ok, Mommy. I love you," Isaiah said and blew her a kiss through the window. Ashley pretended to catch it and put it in her pocket.

"I love you back," Ashley said. "Good night everyone." The family said their goodbyes to Ashley and drove to the gravesite.

I honestly don't remember how we made it home. Constant images played in my mind like a movie teaser as I drove home. Cuts of different scenes flashed through my recent memory. How Mr. Jax lunged toward the casket as it was lowered into the ground; Eric gazing toward the sky, rocking back and forth as streams of tears dived from his face. Kaila confused from it all and still uncertain how to react, looked at everyone else's sadness and grief and mimicked the emotion with fake outbursts and random tantrums.

I bawled the whole ride while Kaila slept soundly. My thoughts turned to whispers that morphed into screams and cuss words. "This is all your fault," I repeated to myself through tears until Kaila and I pulled into the driveway. Kaila slept soundly for nearly an hour, yet the moment the

189

car stopped moving, Kaila sprung awake as if it wasn't nearly midnight. Kaila saw Taylor's car and went ballistic with excitement.

"Mommy came home from heaven," she screamed and ran inside the house. I followed behind her as she scoured every room. "Mom. Mom? Mom!" she shouted. She checked behind the shower curtain in her bathroom, our walk-in closet, even in the jacuzzi on the patio. "Mom?" she whimpered. She settled into disappointment after discovering every room in the house was empty.

She calmed herself by crying until she fell asleep. Eventually, Kaila woke up, howling for her mother's comfort. With Kaila in my arms, I paced the wooden floors enough to drill a hole into the basement. Under the circumstances, I'd kill for two solid hours of uninterrupted sleep. The thirty-minute cat naps and waking up in cold sweats didn't work for my already anxious nerves. I managed to get Kaila into our bed, snuggled up with Taylor's favorite scarf.

Lying in the bed didn't help with my anxiety or put me to sleep. "Maybe a hot shower will help," I thought. I got up slowly, careful not to wake up Kaila. As the water spouted against my back, I became overwhelmed with gut-wrenching sadness and grief. I curled into a ball leaning on the expensive tile we argued about when Taylor wanted to remodel. I cried out for understanding. I didn't get an answer that made sense so I got out of the shower and went back to lay down.

After staring at the black ceiling for another one hour, I reached for my phone on the nightstand. Four forty-four. I scrolled through my recent photos' gallery. Too many selfies not enough usies. I pressed my finger down and dialed voicemail.

"You have one message in your mailbox. Press 1 to hear it," the recording said. I pressed one.

"You could've told me about this but no. You told Ashley. Of all people? Austynn. You know that bitch Austynn only wants my father's money! The money your married into. And now with that new kid of yours she's got full access.
You're so dumb and blinded by your infatuation with her that you can't even see it! I swear I wish I never stayed with you. I wish I never wasted years of my life with you only for you to turn around and betray me like this? I hope you choke on your new life."

I hit repeat. Over and over again. Taylor's last recorded words were harsh, her voice shaky but stern. Every syllable she spoke ripped a piece of my heart out - but the silence was harder to bear.

Ashley
The One

"You've had a few -- one too many, but I'm the only one to wake you up." -
Tamar Braxton

Beep. Beep. Beep. Beep. I glanced at the monitor from the vinyl chair I sat in. Ray returned to the room with a cup of coffee and a brown paper bag. Ray walked over to me, handed me the styrofoam cup and gave me a kiss. He sat down next to me and quietly opened the paper bag.

"I don't want her to wake up," Ray whispered. I nodded. I turned to peek out of the window. The view of the ninth floor overlooked downtown Providence. I could spot Taylor's house and the Blackstone from here. I sighed. "Taylor would disapprove," I thought as I peeked over my shoulder at Alana in the hospital bed. I took a sip of coffee and turned to Ray.

"Are you ready?" I asked him. He smiled and nodded.

"Ready for this to be over," Ray responded. "I'm kind of anxious."

"You'll get all the answers soon enough," I reassured him. I rubbed his arm and sipped my coffee. My entire life did a complete 180 in less than 30 days, yet I jumped back into my daily routine like nothing changed. If I acted normal, things would balance out, I thought to myself. So even though my best friend died a month ago, here I was comforting someone else. It helped to take my mind off of death and focus on life - even if it was uncomfortable for me.

Alana's water broke a week before her due date. She had a tear in her placenta that slowly leaked so she has been on bedrest since. However, today, was the actual birth and I wanted to know just as much as Ray did if he is in fact the father of this child. Reluctantly and at Ray's persistence, I accompanied him to offer moral support.

Alana tossed her head around on the pillow before squinting her eyes open. She yawned and stretched, just as the door opened. A few dozen of latex balloons, a couple of 'Congratulations & It's a Girl' mylar balloons floated into the room as combat boot footsteps followed.

"Hey, Alana. I made it just in time..." a man said. "Ms. Davis told me where to find you." He was dressed in tactical gear. At first glance he looked like he came from a paintball session. I noticed the US flag on his sleeve and the gold lettering of his name on patches. Definitely military. Air force, if I had to guess.

He placed his balloon bouquet in the corner and handed Alana a gift bag, two single-stemmed yellow roses and a box of newborn Pampers.

"Hello everyone," he addressed us. Ray and I exchanged the look. "Who are they?" he whispered to Alana as he squeezed next to her on the twin-sized bed.

"I thought you were going to be away," Alana replied as she propped up and scooted over.

"Me too," he said. "I'm glad I made it though." He leaned in for a kiss.

"Do you care to tell me what happened?" Alana said as she dodged his attempt.

"Who are these people?" He asked again. This time, loud enough for us to hear.

"Focus, Reggie," Alana said. "You weren't supposed to be back until 2022. You know after your Syrian tour."

"Turns out," he said as he grabbed the remote control from Alana's hand. "They didn't need my services after all. It was an honorable discharge - so I still get the perks - but I don't have to go to Syria. I'm back now," he said.

"That's Ray," Alana said. "And that's Ashley."

"So you're Ray," the mystery man said as he grew a devilish grin.

193

"And you are," Ray asked. Reggie was Ray's doppelganger. They shared the same athletic body type and a similar hue. Reggie had darker eyes to Ray's green ones but they were still light. Reggie was about two inches taller than Ray. Everything else - you would've thought they were twins.

"I'm Reggie," the man said as he extended his hand out.

"I'm glad you've been able to take care of my lady while I was away," he said to Ray. Ray looked at his hand then glanced at Alana. Ray shook Reggie's hand. "You'd think she'd be happier to see her man." Reggie laughed then shrugged.

"Wait, Alana is your lady, lady?" I asked, shocked but not surprised. After the stories I've heard and the antics I've witnessed, I'm not surprised at all.

"This is your man?" Ray asked Alana, almost with delight. "I knew it!" He pumped his fists in the air in victory.

"I called Ms. Davis and she told me she was on her way to the hospital. So I showed up to surprise you," Reggie said softly.

"Well, I'm surprised," Alana said. She folded her arms over her big belly. "Remind me to kill my mother please, thanks." Reggie tilted his head back and laughed a deep, back-bending cackle. He eyed Alana, who looked away quickly.

"What am I missing here?" I said. "Is Reggie a Daddy-candidate, too?"

"Oh, so that's the story you decided to go with," Reggie asked.

"You weren't supposed to be here," Alana murmured. Tears welled up in her eyes. She waved her hand in front of her face and breathed heavily.

"Alana isn't having Ray's baby," Reggie revealed. "She was already pregnant with my child the last time you and her had sex."

"Who are you bro," Ray said. "I ain't never heard of you."

"I heard of you though. Even you, Ashley, right? I've dealt with Alana on and off since high school. I left for the Air Force and she went to college. Whenever I get deployed we'd separate, she'll fixate on someone and she'll have her fun until I come back. It went on for years. Last year, when I was deployed in late November, she was already pregnant. She's just been eyeing you for months to be my stand-in."

"Your stand-in?" Ray had a look of disgust on his face.

"As crazy as this girl is about Ray," I said. You telling me none of it was real?"

"Alana only chose Ray because he reminds her of me. Alana is really crazy about me. And it's because I get her. And because I do that thing with my tongue she can't get enough of." Reggie chuckled as he playfully poked into Alana's rib, who giggled after a brief hesitation.

"Wow," I said. Mind. Blown.

"How do you know you're the father," Ray asked. He sounded disappointed. "I need a DNA test, man. This scene and that story proves nothing."

"He's over-exaggerating," Alana interjected. "We were best friends in high school. We fooled around from time to time in college and it continued whenever he came home from deployment but it wasn't ever anything major. Reggie is not my man, and he knows that."

"Oh, so you and Reggie were how you and I were," Ray said. "You were giving out benefits to all your friends, I see."

"It wasn't like that," Alana said.

"Until it was," Reggie said. "We got back together when you decided to marry her," he said as he pointed to me. Alana's lip quivered as she built up the courage to confess. A single tear fell down her left cheek. She sighed and wiped it away.

"Yes. Ok," Alana admitted. "He's right. I got back with him when you decided to propose to Miss Ashley Jay. Everything was Ashley this and Ashley that. I couldn't take it! I kept dealing with you even though I had Reggie because I knew about Ashley and I didn't care," Alana

195

continued. "I wanted you to want me how you want her. And then I found out I was pregnant. With Reggie leaving for four years, I had to make sure my daughter was going to be taken care of. I couldn't get a hold of of you. I really thought the baby was yours."

"So you trapped Ray?" I asked.

"It wasn't a trap," Alana pleaded. "At one point I did think the baby was Ray's. Then Reggie insisted we get a DNA test before he left. And you were with Ashley all the time. I just wanted someone to be there for me."

"You could've asked," I said. "If you and Ray were so cool." Ray didn't open his mouth. He stood idle, in awe. "Why trap Ray?"

"I swear it wasn't a trap. I loved Ray." Alana said with no chagrin.

"But if you were already pregnant - issa trap, boo. You only told him about it and made him think it was his for your own sick benefit. Chicks are really out here trying to ruin a man's happiness. That is evil, personified, honey."

"When you came around, Ray became a different person. Then he never had time for me. Ray never chose me. He chose everyone else though. All the new chicks who came along even though I was right there the whole time. I thought a baby would make him choose me, finally."

"Obviously, I made the right choice," Ray finally spoke. "You were out here being a hoe this whole time."

"Hey," Reggie defended. "Mr. Pot meet Miss Kettle," Reggie said. "You've got some nerve." Reggie stepped to Ray. Ray and Reggie were chest to chest, staring at each other.

"Easy fellas, let's not do this here. There's a baby coming into this world and it needs to be a peaceful environment. So cut it out," I demanded.

"I still think a DNA test is necessary," Ray said. "To be 100% sure." Alana shook her head and buried her face in the palm of her hands. Reggie pulled out a folded piece of paper from one of his cargo pants

196

pockets. He handed it to Ray.

"I'm 100% sure that you are not the father," Reggie said as Ray read over the paper. Ray gave it to me.

"I guess he could afford the CVS test?" Ray said. I read it thoroughly. And threw the paper at Alana, who laughed, nervously. She tensed up, balled her fists and started to hyperventilate.

"We should go," I said to Ray. Alana was having a contraction. He walked out the door without saying another word. I walked toward the door and looked back. Reggie sat behind Alana to rub her back. He kissed her neck and whispered in her ear. Whatever he said made her smile. I left shaking my head. I met Ray at the elevator. The doors opened as soon as I got in front of the double doors.

"Better him than me, I tell you," he said. "I never met crazy like that before." We stepped inside and both laughed. Ray pulled me into a hug.

"Thank you," Ray said.

"For what?" I asked.

"Being born," he replied.

"You are so extra," I said to him. "But I like it."

"I know you do," Ray said. "I keep telling you, I'm trying to have forever with you, girl."

Three Months Later

The day finally arrived. The sunshine danced through the tall, glass window of the Omni Hotel suite as temperatures pushed upward toward the mid-fifties. Not too bad for a New England December. I glanced over at the nightstand and debated if I wanted to answer my phone vibrating relentlessly. I knew it was Morgan or Jasmin with another question about the party later.

I did not bother to check to see who called. I needed time to relax after the hour long walkthrough with Ray and the wedding coordinator. Ray walked behind me the entire tour. He made faces behind the coordinator's back, humped my backside, slapped the air, pinched my cheeks and caressed any visible part of my body, with that look in his eye. I could tell Ray was more excited for the wedding night than the ceremony but as long as we get through it, he'll get a wedding night he deserves.

As Ray's friends gathered for his bachelor party in the suite adjacent to mine, I took some time to relax in the jacuzzi. I noticed I only had an hour before the hotel staff prepared the decor and setup for my carnival-themed bachelorette party.

As I ran the water for the jacuzzi to heat up, my phone rang again on the nightstand. I ignored it again and jumped in the jacuzzi. About ten minutes into my alone-time, I heard a knock at the door.

"Someone decided to show up early..." I thought as I grabbed a robe to answer the door. The knocks increased as I got closer. "I'm coming" I said. I wrapped a towel around my head and skipped to answer the door.

"What are you doing here?" I asked. "How did you know I was here?"

"I needed to find you before you make the biggest mistake of your life."

"Ugh, Travis, really?" I couldn't believe that Travis was standing before mre, the night before my wedding day.

"I am really here," he said. "To ask for a second chance."

"A second chance at what? You breaking my heart?"

"I realized it should have been you all along and I just want the chance to prove it."

"I'm sorry it took you so long to see I was always in your corner."

"I know and that's why I'm here. I need you to know I want us to try again."

"What in the Aaliyah, dust-yourself-off-and-try-again voodu nonsense are you talking about? I'm getting married tomorrow."

"Don't marry him. Marry me."

"I'm not sure if you know but Ray is right next door. If he sees this," I said. "He'll call off the wedding, himself." Travis stepped back and looked down the hall, first to his left then to the right.

"Which room? I'll tell him myself," Travis said. He walked toward the left. I pulled his arm back.

"Are you crazy?" I said as I pulled him into my hotel room.

"I just want you to remember us. How we were. What we talked about. I want you to think about us before you marry Ray."

"I can't even believe I'm entertaining this, but please tell me how you came to this revelation?" I guided Travis to the round table and we both sat down. He scooped my hands into his. When I pulled away he reached for it again. Travis wouldn't let my hand go. He stared at my engagement ring and began to fiddle with it.

"I really want you to take that ring off," he said.

"I really want to know why you show up at my hotel room, a day before I'm getting married to ask for a second chance. What happened to Corrine and Mia?"

"I told them both I couldn't be with them because I wanted to be with you."

"How do you figure you want to be with me though? I still have the same problem you claim was the reason why you couldn't be with me."

"I know and I should have been more compassionate about that. I realize now."

"Now is too late."

"Sometimes people have to go through things to realize who's really for them. I went through some things with both of them and they don't compare to how I felt with you. I'm trying to see if we can get that back and grow."

"Travis," I said when I heard another knock at the door. "This trip down memory lane is killing me right now." I got up to answer it and there were a vase full of flowers and a little white box on the floor. I turned to Travis, who smiled and shrugged. I reached down to pick them up and brought them to the table.

"Listen, I don't want to have to come to the ceremony tomorrow, in front of hundreds of people, to interrupt your wedding during the infamous 'if anyone objects speak now.' part," Travis said.

"Please don't," I replied.

"But I will," he insisted. I opened the box and it was a ring inside. I shook my head and closed the box. I slid it across the table.

"You know I'm getting married tomorrow," I said softly. "Because I love Ray."

"I know you love me, too," Travis said with confidence. "And I'm ready now."

"Well, maybe you're just ready now - to be with someone else," I said. "I will always love you, Travis. I just know that you only come around when things are going right for you. I give you comfort, a little ego boost and I'm back to being alone while you live it up with another chick. But when I needed you the most, when Taylor passed, you weren't there. And that told me all I needed to know."

Travis slid the ring box back to me, stood up and pulled me into a hug. His big arms and chest covered me like a warm blanket. The embrace lasted long. Every time I pulled back he held me tighter.

"I know you feel it," he said. Travis gazed into my eyes in search of the love I once had for him.

"I feel something," I said as he put me down. I laughed. He chuckled and instantly became bashful.

"You do it to me every time," he said. Travis stared at me, still holding my hand. "I just don't want you to forget about us and how easy our situation was. I miss that. I miss you."

He leaned down, our foreheads touching, and went in for a kiss. Travis touched the small of my back and pulled me closer. His soft lips sucked me in. My heart raced. He lifted me in the air and wrapped my legs around his waist. We spun around. Kissing. Lip-biting. Tongue. Heavy breathing. I pulled away with a magnetic resistance.

"See," Travis said with a smile as he walked toward the door. "You can't deny that feeling right there. I want you to feel that, forever. Call me tonight...or I'll see you tomorrow."

"Travis," I said softly.

"I'm serious, Ashley," he said as he left my hotel room. Just as Travis left me with so many unanswered questions, the hotel staff passed him in the hall with all the party decor to bring my idea to life.

While the reception decor was sparkling table covers, crystal chandeliers and with 24 inch vases of hydrangeas, the bachelorette party was going to be laid back. An old-fashioned popcorn maker, a cotton candy machine, skee ball and ring toss game were set up in the suite. Along with two small tables for Spades and Blackjack, with a stocked bar of my favorite brown, Hennessy.

Guests began to arrive quickly, one after the other. Morgan was the first guest to show. Jasmin and my mother, RIta showed up together, while a few of my work friends arrived later. They gathered in the den area. Gift boxes and bags piled onto a gift table in the corner. Drinks included cotton candy cocktails and root beer floats. The appetizers were fried dough, different toppings, from marinara sauce and Parmesan cheese, shrimp ceviche, and caviar, pretzels, nachos and cheese.

"Taylor would be happy to see this," Miss Amy said as she arrived with her luscious box of treats. She removed her soft fur coat that draped to the floor. She was dripped in diamonds and designer couture. "So quaint. Low-key. Laid-back. This is cute," she said. She leaned in for a hug as the butler removed her fur. "Be careful with that."

"I know you miss her. We all do, but it's Ashley's night. Please can we let it be about her?" Morgan asked as politely as she could muster.

"You're right, Morgan," she said. "My apologies." Miss Amy grabbed a glass from the mini bar and pulled a gold champagne bottle out of her Chanel bag. Miss Amy sat back on the leather side chair and poured herself multiple servings.

We played games, won prizes and laughed harder than we did in months. Dinner was served and we ate a little fancier than the appetizers. Grilled lobster tail with garlic butter sauces set atop mashed potatoes and asparagus, shrimp scampi alfredo pasta, tomato bisque with crabmeat, stuffed clams, a Caesar salad awaited us as suited waiters served our meal. We had small talk about honeymoons, catching flights and where to dine while in Paris.

After dinner, the party gathered around to open gifts. Most of the gifts I opened was lingerie and bedroom candy. I reached for one with a purple bow and smile as I opened it. Ray sent the first photo of us together, framed. The second frame was empty with a slot for every five year increment. I opened a gift bag Morgan handed to me with a photo album. The first page had a note in it that said:

> "For every year in between. One day we'll give to our grandkids
> so they can see what love looks like."

"Is it weird if I congratulate you on hitting the marriage jackpot?" Morgan asked me.

"Extremely," I replied. "You're not even a fan of marriage."

"Exactly. That's why I think y'all are so bomb. Like...there aren't too many 'reformed' players out there. It's refreshing to see someone actually be who they say they are. Ray changed for you and it shows."

"Ray has been pretty consistent, I must admit," I said.

"And he loves you. Like worships you. You can see the love in his eyes. It's beautiful."

"I know. It's nice, isn't it," I said. "It's nice to feel."

We finished the night up with more laughs and made new memories. As everyone wished me a good night, and grabbed their belongings to leave, I reminded them of the next day's attire: formal wear.

"No bodycon dresses or minis. Think damn near evening gowns. Please. I don't want to have to kick you out on my wedding day for your clothes," I said as I gifted everyone with cupcake cocktail shots as prizes. Morgan helped hand out the remaining treats.

"You sound like Taylor," Morgan said. "She would love to be the fashion police at anybody's wedding."

"I know, right," I said. I sighed. "She's going to miss a good show."

"She sure is," Morgan said. "But she's watching. From up above." Morgan and I looked at each other then the floor. "Well…"

"Morgan, I can't with you," I said laughing.

"Too soon? I know…I'm sorry, I couldn't help it. I'm sure wherever she is she wishes you the best."

"I wish she was here to see it," I said.

"Don't be sad about it. You can't change God's plan," Morgan said. "Just remember the good times and move on."

"Morgan, my new voice of reason," I said.

"Always here for you, friend," Morgan said. "Now, rest up. You have a wedding to star in."

Last night was magic, filled with fairy dust and starlights. I woke up groggy, with a headache that made the soft music playing sound like the Energizer bunny on steroids with a new battery in its back. Is that the Jackson 5? It reminded me of when Harold would make breakfast for the family on Sunday mornings. I rolled over and opened one eye to check the time. One minute before my alarm went off, blasting Blaze 101. I stuffed my face back in the pillow, then a phone rang.

"Hello," I said groggily. I reached for every button to stop the noise.

"Wake up, beautiful. Are you ready for today?"

"Yes I am! I just woke up. I still feel hungover."

"We had one hell of a night last night. It's going to be an even better night tonight."

"I know I can't wait," I said as I perked up.

"You sound more excited than usual for Mr. Jax's annual Christmas Celebration."

"Eric?" I said, rubbing my eyes.

"The one and only. You sound surprised."

"I am. I haven't heard from you in ages," I said as I leaned against the headboard. "Last night is a little fuzzy. Is Isaiah ok?"

"Who is Isaiah? That's a nice name."

"You are funny," I said as I became a little more coherent. "Acting like you don't know Isaiah. Where is he?"

"I don't know who Isaiah is," Eric said. "Should I?"

"Yes. You should. Are you having one of your episodes?"

"Ashley, what are you talking about? Episodes? Are you cheating on me or something?"

"Oh. My. God. Eric. No. I'm not cheating on you," I chuckled. "What year do you think it is? 2008?" Eric laughed.

"Yes, I do. Because it is. And it will be for at least another two weeks."

"Right. Whatever you say. Can I at least say hi to our son?"

"Are you trying to tell me something? I mean, I know I was hitting it right last night, but how would you know that you're pregnant already?"

"Eric, it sounds like you need your meds. Really? Last night I was at a hotel party."

"I know. I got it for us to celebrate your birthday. You don't remember I dropped you off early morning so our parents wouldn't be upset. Did the champagne get to you *that* much?"

"I did have a lot to drink last night," I admitted. "But you're describing something that happened ages ago. Are you sure you haven't had your medication?"

"Medication? I'm starting to think you need something. How's your head? You did bang it on your way inside last night. You're really starting to make me nervous. Where's Miss Rita and Jasmin? Is Harold there? Do you need to look at a calendar or something. Maybe someone should take you to get check out."

"I know it's my birthday. I also know I'm supposed to be getting married today," I said. I looked down at my left hand and my ring was gone. I looked around the trinkets on my four-drawer chest. I moved things around on the nightstand. I checked my closet for the jacket I had wore the night before. I searched the jewelry box I keep under my bed. It was nowhere to be found.

"Where is my ring?" I asked out loud in frustration.

"What ring? Did you lose your mom's ring?"

"No. My engagement ring," I said, confused.

205

"You didn't even give me a chance to propose," Eric said.

"What are you talking about? We've been down this road before," I said still glancing around the room.

"You're still in school with nearly two semesters left. I thought we could wait for you to finish. I mean, I guess I can get you a ring now," Eric said. The more Eric talked the more he confused me. And being unable to find my ring made me cry real tears. I couldn't understand what was going on.

"Eric, I know this is hard for you to comprehend, but it isn't 2008. It's 2018. I get your time lapse, ok. It's cool. I'll call Miss Amy to get Isaiah."

"Miss Amy knows Isaiah?"Eric asked. "Should I be worried?" He laughed, nervously.

"Ok. Eric. I guess I'll catch up with you later," I said in my most polite tone. Eric started to say something else but my attention shifted to the radio announcer.

"Merry Christmas Eve everybody, It's your boy Manny Money. It's December 24, 2008 and I am new to the airwaves! Bear with me as I bring you the most bomb radio show you've ever heard. Hit me up o the phone lines, tell me what you want to hear. I'm dropping the first throwback hit of the night, the Notorious B.I.G.'s Juuuuuicccyyyyyyyy! Christmas won't miss us this year! Let's go!"

The beat dropped and the lyrics started to play as I froze in front of the mirror. I spun around in disbelief as the realization set in. Birthday balloons filled my room as it did every year when I stayed with my parents. My younger sister, Jasmin, always bought me dozen balloons to celebrate my birthday because that's all she could afford when we were younger; it became tradition.

My twin size bed had the same leopard print bedspread like the one I had in college. The oversized teddy bear Eric won for me at our senior trip to the carnival was plopped in the corner. On my dresser were framed pictures of Taylor and I throughout the years. Her arm over mine, standing shoulder-to-shoulder in turtlenecks and high-waisted jeans. Eighth grade dance, high school prom pictures, collages of our college years were posted on the wall.

If it were really 2008, Harold will come in with my birthday breakfast, French toast topped with fresh strawberries and whipped cream with a side of scrambled cheese eggs and swine bacon, as he did every year.

"Um Eric. Hello," I said as I gripped the cordless phone.

"Yes Ashley. Are you ok?" Eric asked.

Four months prior to my wedding day, in 2019, Taylor, my best friend, Eric's sister, Isaiah's aunt, and Kaila's mom, died. A drunk driver hit Taylor's SUV while she sat parked on the side of the road, during Hurricane Florence, a Category 4. She wasn't located for 48 hours after, and no one even suspected that she was missing. Her car was found overturned past the woods, shoreside of a shallow river.

"Do you think dreams are real?" I asked.

"I think they could be," Eric said. I became fidgety and paced the room. I shook my hands as they began to tingle. *If Eric wasn't having an episode, then Taylor would be here.* When I realized what happened I couldn't hold my tongue. Last night, I fell asleep thinking it was my wedding day, well into 2019 and I woke up to the year 2008?

I cut him off mid-sentence.

"Eric. Where's Taylor? Let me talk to Taylor, now," I said in a rushed voice. Eric put me on hold for a moment as I waited for confirmation that I wasn't as crazy as Eric was.

"Hey best friend." I heard on the other end of the phone as it dropped out of my hand. I sank into a ball on the floor as I choked on the frog in my throat. I couldn't breath. Trembling with tears streaming down my face, I heard her voice again. "Hello." I heard Taylor say. "Ashley Jay, are you there?"

"So none of it was real," I said with a shaky voice. "It was all a dream?" I recalled as a rush of recent memories ran through my head. "Eric didn't have a mental breakdown? There was never a Jay-J, which means I don't have it! No Travis. No miscarriage? No Ray. No wedding? Oh my god! What about Isaiah? And Taylor, you're alive!" I rambled as tears of joy streamed down my face.

"Of course I am. Where else would I be? What are you babbling about - and are you crying?" Taylor asked.

"I missed you," I said through the tears. "So much!" There was a light knock at the door before it creaked open. Harold walked in with a breakfast plate. He placed it on the foot of my bed and left the room quickly. I was speechless. "Is it really 2008?"

"Yes. Are you ok, Ashley Jay?" Taylor said. "Wait. I'm going to have to go. Miss Amy wants me to help her with dinner before I go see my mom at the hospital. You are going to come tonight, right? I know it's your birthday but you always spend Christmas Eve with us. Eric been really weird lately - talking about the future a lot. But he's also been eating edibles like they're candy. But come. Please. For your best friend."

"I'll be there, Taylor," I said. "I wouldn't miss it for the world."

"Ok. Let me go. I'll see you soon. Are you sure you're ok?" Taylor asked again. I sat on the edge of the bed in awe.

"I can't believe it," I said to Taylor. "I'm just glad you're here, and all of it was just a dream," I said.

"You have to tell me more about this dream of yours," Taylor said. "Please fill me in later!" I beamed on the other end of the phone.

"No doubt," I said. "Prepare to be amazed," I said before we hung up. "Wow!" I said out loud. "I am completely blown away. It was just a dream. Thank God!"

The End

ABOUT THE AUTHOR

Tashema Chanel has been writing professionally since 2006. She has experience in print and digital media. Tashema Chanel has written for the following industries: healthcare, music, fashion, real estate and business.

Triumphs & Tragedies is the finale of the "Love & Lies" book trilogy by Tashema Chanel. The first and second books, *Ignorance Is Bliss*, and *Stuck On Stupid*, are available in print and digital on tashemachanel.com.

www.ingramcontent.com/pod-product-compliance
Lightning Source LLC
Chambersburg PA
CBHW032145020726
47496CB00003B/729